UNANIMO
LYNN S. H
ELAKI I

"ONE OF THE BEST N̶E̶W̶ ̶S̶E̶R̶I̶E̶S̶ ̶I̶N̶ ̶T̶H̶E̶ ̶G̶E̶N̶R̶E̶!"
—*Science Fiction Chronicle*

ALIEN BLUES
**The smash debut novel—introducing homicide
detective David Silver and String, the partner from
another planet . . .**

"An exciting, science-fictional police procedural with truly
alien aliens . . . an absorbing, well-written book."
—*Aboriginal Science Fiction*

"Hightower takes the setup and delivers a grittily realistic
and down-and-dirty serial killer novel . . . impressive . . . a
very promising first novel."　　　　　　　　　　—*Locus*

"Not only are Hightower's aliens truly alien—her cops are
actually human! A high-spirited and spooky new *The
Silence of the Lambs* with otherworldly overtones."
—Terry Bisson, author of *Voyage to the Red Planet*

"Brilliantly entertaining. I recommend it highly. A
crackerjack novel of police detection and an evocative
glimpse of a possible future."
—Nancy Pickard, bestselling author of *IOU*

Turn the page for more rave reviews . . .

ALIEN EYES

The exciting return of homicide detective David Silver and his Elaki partner, String—a shocking case of interstellar violence brought to a new battleground: Earth . . .

"*Alien Eyes* is a page-turner . . . fun, fast-moving . . . a police procedural in a day-after-tomorrow world."
—*Lexington Herald-Leader*

"Hightower takes elements of cyberpunk and novels about a benevolent alien invasion and combines them with the gritty realism of a police procedural to make stories that are completely her own . . . a believable future with a believable alien culture . . . interesting settings, intriguing ideas, fascinating characters [and] a high level of suspense!"
—*Fort Knox Turret*

"Complex . . . snappy . . . original."
—*Asimov's Science Fiction*

"The sequel to the excellent *Alien Blues* [is] a very fine SF novel . . . I'm looking forward to the next installment!"
—*Science Fiction Chronicle*

. . . and don't miss . . .

ALIEN HEAT

Silver and String are back, investigating arsonists and interstellar real-estate investors who may well be part of a massive, bizarre cult . . .

Ace Books by Lynn S. Hightower

ALIEN BLUES
ALIEN EYES
ALIEN HEAT
ALIEN RITES

Alien Rites

Lynn S. Hightower

ACE BOOKS, NEW YORK

Excerpt from *Evidence* by Luc Sante copyright © 1992 by Luc Sante. Reprinted by permission of Farrar, Straus & Giroux, Inc.

This book is an Ace original edition, and has never been previously published.

ALIEN RITES

An Ace Book / published by arrangement with the author

PRINTING HISTORY
Ace edition / July 1995

ISBN: 0-441-00219-6

ACE®
Ace Books are published by The Berkley Publishing Group, 200 Madison Avenue, New York, NY 10016.
ACE and the "A" design are trademarks belonging to Charter Communications, Inc.

PRINTED IN THE UNITED STATES OF AMERICA

10 9 8 7 6 5 4 3 2 1

32752838

To my brother, Jay Christopher,
who's one of my best buddies.
I'm glad we didn't kill each other
while we were growing up.

Acknowledgments

Many thanks to my editor, the talented Ginjer Buchanan, who could not have been kinder or more understanding during a difficult year.

To Norm Golibersuch, Jeff Darling, Mike Reynolds, and Jim Lyon, of the law firm Lyon, Golibersuch, Darling, and Reynolds, who were not only invaluable in helping me with research, but are great fun to hang out with, even if they do sweat when they eat.

To C. William Swinford, attorney-at-law, for consideration, kindness, and setting me free.

To the Singapore gang, Chuck, Bryan, Rebecca, Jay, and Terry, who made a working vacation more fun than I had any business having.

To the Laurel Lake gang, Sam, Mary Audrey, Dee, Bryan and Jerri Powers, Chuck, and Bryan—thanks for feeding me, taking me to the best spots in one of the most beautiful places on earth, and showing me where the bodies are stashed.

To my wonderful agent, Matt Bialer, a closet Elaki.

And, of course, to the world's best support team, Alan, Laurel, and Rachel.

The terrible gift that the dead make to the living is that of sight, which is to say foreknowledge; in return they demand memory, which is to say acknowledgment.

—Luc Sante, *Evidence*

Alien Rites

ONE

DAVID'S STOMACH SANK WHEN HE SAW THE SPATTERS OF brown blood in the front seat of the car. He had hoped, for no particular reason, that there might still be a chance of finding Luke Cochran alive. The uniform leaned over his shoulder, rain coursing down the slicker over his arm. He pointed his light, adding to the dim thread of brightness from the overhead dome.

"She identified the shoe."

David looked at the dirty white tennis shoe—an Eckler, expensive brand. Cochran was a big kid, over six feet, and the shoe looked a size eleven. The laces were frayed, and there was a wad of pink bubble gum stuck to the sole. It was wedged in the hinge of the front seat door, passenger's side, as if Cochran's foot had caught and been wrenched free, leaving the shoe behind.

Someone moving the body?

David ducked out of the open door, head exposed to the downpour of warm, fat rain. "Gotten a statement from the car yet?"

Cochran's car was a sleek, shiny black Visck. It had been pristine and beautiful before it jumped the guardrail and went over the side of the exit ramp into the weed-choked thicket. Raindrops beaded on a paint job that still shone.

David backed into a tangle of sticker vines, tearing the skin across the back of his hand. Rain-diluted blood ran down his fingers. He wiped his hand absently across the back of his jeans, and tripped over an empty, dirt-encrusted carton of Jack Daniels.

The uniform put a hand out. "Steady, sir."

David took a second look at the fleshy young face of the embryo in uniform. His ego plummeted. *Steady, sir?*

He slogged through knee-high weeds to take a look at

the car from the other side. He was wet enough not to care how much more rain he absorbed. The generator on the Crime Scene Unit's van throbbed, someone shouted "Lights," and the car was suddenly bathed in bright yellow illumination.

The light turned everything sordid.

The exit ramp ran with water, coursing over a sodden grey diaper, and the pitted asphalt shimmered with the reflected glow of light. The ragged remains of a pale pink dress circled a guardrail support. David glanced over his shoulder, down the hill toward Elaki-Town. The street lights were dark here at four A.M., and the storefronts, antique stalls, small bars, and restaurants were dark humps at the bottom of the hill.

David wondered about that. No light at all? He was sure the storefronts and restaurants usually stayed lighted. Didn't they?

A car made a shark pass on the main drag, catching the hulking presence of Elaki in its headlights. David hoped the car doors were locked tight, shrugged his shoulders at anyone foolish enough to be in Elaki-Town this time of night. He wondered if he'd be called to a fresh crime scene at the bottom of the hill before he was finished with the one at hand.

He looked back at the dark streets, sensing the Elaki backed up into the storefronts. Watching, he supposed—the carnival of red and blue lights, vans, ambulances. Human drama. He was wondering where the hell Mel and String were, when he caught sight of the girl.

She stood on the exit ramp under a street light, as if seeking warmth. Her shoulders sagged low, feet turned inward—pigeon-toed, elbows out. She was worrisomely thin, arms bony and bare and running with rain. Her electric-blue tank top had a high collar, and her jeans were threadbare, sagging under the weight of water absorbed. She clutched a large bundle of blankets to her chest, and her eyes were closed.

The bundle in her arms moved, and David realized that she held a small child, a toddler, no more than two or three.

He looked at the uniform and pointed. "Who is that?"

"Oh. That's her."

"Her?"

"The one all the fuss was about, who poisoned her newborn baby. Annie Trey."

She did not look old enough to be out after curfew. David moved toward her, noting that the technicians, uniforms, and detectives kept a constant distance from this small young girl, as if she were contaminated. He counted five large umbrellas. Four empty cars. And no one had offered to shelter this child with a child from the wet and the dark.

The baby coughed, sounding croupy, emitting a small cry heavy with misery. The girl tucked the small head under her chin, tightened her grip, and cooed softly. She did not open her eyes. She bent forward, as if her back ached, and David wondered how long she had stood there, holding the child.

TWO

ANNIE TREY OPENED HER EYES WHEN HE APPROACHED, large blue eyes. Her hair was chin-length and dark, wet and close on her scalp. There was a nasty scab on one cheek, and her lashes were brown and thin. The freckles on her nose and cheeks were faint enough that you couldn't see them unless you got close.

David did not think he had ever seen anyone who gave so strong an impression of being separate and alone.

Annie Trey had been much in the news—the unwed mother of an eighteen-month-old daughter, and a newborn son who died at three weeks of a violent and mysterious ailment that was toxic, swift, and unkind. She had not yet been indicted, except by the media, but there was talk of poison, and a simmering outrage that the toddler was still in her care.

As far as David knew, the case was still under investigation. Public opinion was unsympathetic. Annie Trey was not pretty. She was below average in intelligence. She was not married, though she had admitted wistfully on the evening news that she'd like to be. She was from the South, somewhere small and obscure in Mississippi. She was quoted saying things like "being done dirt."

People did not like to think that newborn babies could die suddenly, painfully, and unexpectedly without someone to blame. Even those who were objective enough to reserve judgment could not help thinking there must be some reason the newspapers were after this Trey girl. And if Annie Trey had indeed poisoned her child, horrible as that might be, the tragedy kept its distance. Pregnant women could rest easier knowing such a thing could not happen to their babies.

David held out a hand. "Let's get you and your little

one out of the rain, shall we?''

She looked at him. Blinked.

"I'm Detective Silver. David."

It took another beat for the words to sink in, and even then, she was wary. She inclined her head toward a knot of uniforms and detectives next to a patrol car.

"They said I had to stay." Her voice was in the upper registers, sharp around the edges.

David's jaw went tight, but he smiled. "Not in the rain, you don't. Let's get your baby out of this wind."

She thought a minute, then nodded and followed him to his car, which he'd left parked in the middle of the exit ramp. The headlights cast strips of illumination across her wet jeans. Drops of rain jittered in the light.

David opened the passenger door, motioned her in. He reached for the baby. She paused, looked at him carefully, and handed him the child. The father in him applauded her caution.

He peeped under the blanket, careful not to expose the child's head.

A beauty, this little girl. Eyes big and brown, fat black curls damp and wiry. She had sweet, fine, baby skin, flushed red now, with fever. The tiny button nose dripped, and David wiped it clean with his handkerchief.

The baby coughed, croupy and deep. David handed her to her mother and closed the door on the rain. He opened the trunk of the car, found a thick blue towel, worn but clean, opened the driver's door.

Annie Trey took the towel, head cocked to one side, eyes narrow, while he gave instructions to the car.

"Ms. Trey and her baby will be sitting here for now. Please stay put and let Ms. Trey instruct you as to heat and comfort." He smiled at the girl, who was only a few years older than his own Kendra. "Be right back." He glanced over his shoulder, resisted the urge to tell her to lock the doors. She should be safe, cops everywhere you looked.

He had not recognized the woman in the beige raincoat, and he studied her as he approached the cluster of detectives. She was short and stocky, built like a large dwarf, not unattractive, hair short, thick, and swingy. Her eyes were brown, carefully made up, eyebrows thick.

She stood next to Vincent Thurmon, Detective, Missing Persons. This one David knew. He held out a hand.

"Vince?"

"David? I heard you caught this one. Didn't recognize you down there."

They shook hands, Thurmon squinting through reddened blue eyes. The lenses of his eyes were milky and opaque—no surprise he hadn't known David till he was close enough to touch. Seven years ago he'd disarmed a man threatening yet another MacDonalds, eyes powder-burned in the struggle as the gun went off in his face. It was a freaky thing—the bullet missed him entirely, but his eyes were seriously infected by the time he made it through the clogged health-care system. The routing physician made a miscall—not terribly unusual. Thurmon had lost sixty-five percent of his vision.

"I guess this is your baby now," Thurmon said. "Let me know how I can help."

David nodded, frowning. Definitely alcohol on the man's breath. Maybe he'd been off duty when the call came in. As always, he wore a hat, and water had beaded on the brim. He motioned for David to come under the umbrella.

David shrugged. "Can't get much wetter than I am already."

"Where is Annie?" This from the woman in the beige raincoat.

David gave her a second look, knowing that both she and Thurmon had watched while he settled the girl and her child in his car. Perhaps this was her way of muscling into the conversation.

He ignored her. "I don't have much background on this, Thurmon."

Thurmon nodded. "Came in as a 911 five days ago."

"Tuesday," David said.

The woman grinned, friendly. "Very good, Detective. Tuesday was five days ago."

Thurmon waved a hand. "This is Angie Nassif. She's—"

"I'm a social worker. Annie's one of mine."

One of mine. David did not like the way she said it. He gave her a stiff nod, thinking this was the one who had turned Annie in for investigation. Realized he was taking sides way too early in the game.

"If I look familiar, it's probably because you've seen me on the news." Her grin had a sort of gamine, chipmunk quality. Which was not reason enough to dislike her as much as he did.

Cops and social workers, he thought. Oil and water.

"Why are you here?" David asked.

Her mouth opened; then she shrugged. "I'm here to look after Annie. And the child, of course."

She was standing uphill, but was short enough that he still looked down at her. "You must have just gotten here, Ms. Nassif. You'll be relieved to know that Ms. Trey and her baby are safe in my car. Out of the rain and the wind."

She had a clear, dusky complexion. The blush spread from the neckline of the tight white Peter Pan collar on the silk blouse, up the short neck, across the powdered cheeks.

It shut her up.

David turned back to Thurmon. "Who made the call? The 911."

"Annie . . . uh, Ms. Trey. Said she was on the phone to this kid, Luke Cochran, and he said something about somebody messing with his car, and he'd be right back." Thurmon belched discreetly into his fist.

"Then what?" David said.

"She waited on the phone a while, but he never came back. So she called the police."

David frowned. "Why'd she call the police?"

"What?"

"Most people would assume they were cut off."

"Phone told her he'd left the room. He didn't come back. We sent a patrol car out. Car and the kid both gone." Thurmon shrugged. "So. He left her hanging, not a criminal offense. All things considered, we didn't make too much of it."

No, David thought. Someone like Annie Trey worried

about a boyfriend. Not a ripple.

"Anybody seen him since?"

Thurmon shrugged. "Not sure."

Didn't check, David thought. "There's blood in the car."

Thurmon grimaced. "I heard. Look, Silver, I'll send you my file. A recording of the 911 thing. Anything else—"

"I'll let you know." David shook the man's hand.

Thurmon turned away, then looked back over his shoulder. "We've got a hell of a workload, Silver. And you know how they are."

"They?"

"Women."

David nodded.

"Angie, I give you a ride?" Thurmon asked.

"No, I think I'll stick around." She stood on tiptoe, trying to look over David's shoulder.

He turned, saw the first yellow van that meant media.

"Detective Silver?"

"Yes, Ms. Nassif?"

"Are you going to be questioning Annie?"

He looked at her, said nothing.

She stood up straighter. "Maybe I should come along."

"Why?"

"Pardon?"

"Why should you come along?"

"Well . . . I . . ." Her eyes went narrow. "Most police officers cooperate with my department, Officer."

"Sooner or later everybody runs out of luck." David jammed his hands in his pockets, headed down the exit ramp to his car. He wondered why he'd declared out and out war with Social Services. As if he didn't have enough to worry about.

THREE

———————————
———

THE BABY WAS DRY AND SLEEPY, HEAD ON HER MOTHER'S shoulder. Annie Trey had used the towel to buffer the child from her drenched shirt and jeans. David slid wetly into the driver's seat of the car and looked on approvingly, judging Annie's motherhood, as if he had the right.

The air in the car was sweaty and thick, the windows fogged. David took a deep breath of stuffy air, inhaling the milky soft smell of baby mixed with the camphor odor of cough medicine. A sticky orange film leaked from the corner of the child's mouth. The same stuff he gave his kids.

The baby coughed, eyes flicking open, then rolling back as she settled again in sleep.

"Medicine helping?" David asked.

Annie Trey hugged the child close to her chest. "Not so you'd notice. Sometimes it takes a while."

"How long's she been sick?" David asked gently.

Annie looked away, voice toneless. "I took her in to the clinic soon as she got a runny nose. Ms. Nassif can tell you."

David met her eyes. She looked hunted. In spite of the lack of emotion in her voice, her hands were shaking.

David patted her shoulder. "I need to ask you some questions, but I think you better get that baby tucked into bed. Would it be all right if I have a patrol officer drive you home, and stop by later tonight, or early tomorrow morning? It's important I talk to you right away."

"Do you think he's dead?" It was a small voice, and weary.

David looked at her, hesitated. He wondered what had caused the wound on her cheek, wondered how she would look without the brownish-red scab. He could not imagine her looking pretty.

"They showed me Luke's shoe." Her lower lip trembled.

David kept his voice steady and gentle, and did not look away when she gave him the mingled look of hope and dawning horror that was always so hard to watch.

"Ms. Trey, I don't know anything definite yet. But he hasn't been seen or heard from in—"

"Five days," she said.

David nodded. "The shoe isn't a good sign. I wish I could tell you one way or the other, but I don't know enough yet, and we haven't had a chance to interview the car."

"But—"

He waited. She frowned, hugged the baby close. If she wanted more, she'd ask for it. He'd learned to let people take things at their own pace.

Her hair was drying on top—fine, flat, flyaway hair. She tried to pull a piece into her mouth, but it didn't quite reach.

New hair cut, David thought. Stylish, but wrong for the round, lightly freckled face.

She looked at him, a hard look for a kid this young. "Do you think Luke's dead? Do you *think* he is?"

"I think you should be prepared for bad news."

She nodded and swallowed and gave him an empty smile that made him wince. Women would always smile, no matter what. He wondered what it did to their insides. Annie Trey looked away, wiping the foggy window with the back of her hand. "Is there a bus stop around here?"

David looked over his shoulder at Elaki-Town, dark and heavy behind them at the end of the exit.

"No."

"There's got to—"

"No," he said again. "Not safe, and the two of you don't need to get any wetter. I'll get somebody to drive you home."

Her jaw went hard and she turned sideways, facing him. "They stare at me. Whoever, whatever person you get to carry me back. They stare and won't say a word. Except some of them, they say awful things. And even if they don't, I worry they will.''

David looked at her. "How old are you?"

Her eyes widened, then dulled. She was used to impertinent questions. ''Nineteen.''

"You don't need to get . . . what's your baby's name?"

''Jenny. She's not a baby, she's almost two.''

They were both babies, David thought, but knew better than to say so. Unkind to take her dignity, especially when that looked to be all she had.

"You need to take Jenny home to bed. She doesn't need to be out waiting for a bus, and this is a bad area."

"No worse than where I live."

David nodded. "But you know your way around there, and you know not to be out alone this time of night. Right?''

Her shoulders sagged. "Okay."

It was a little test, to make sure she put the baby's welfare before her own in all things, including pride. David looked at her and saw a good mother.

He'd seen good mothers do terrible things.

Had she poisoned her infant? And if she had, was she a garden variety sociopath, or had she been driven by horrors he did not understand?

"Stay put," he said. He locked her in the car, feeling silly, but unable to shake that feeling of menace.

FOUR

DAVID RECOGNIZED THE VAN—POLICE ISSUE—PARKED AT
an angle behind the lone yellow media truck. He looked
for his partner. A reporter scanned the area, a flat, uninter-
ested look on his face. He scratched the back of his head,
said something to the technician.

Too small a crime for a media van. David wondered why
they were there. And if they'd bother to stay.

"Pack up," the reporter said loudly.

David nodded, satisfied. One less problem. He hoped
they wouldn't get a glimpse of Annie Trey before they left.
Her presence would stir things up.

He saw a movement from the corner of his eye—Angie
Nassif coming in from the left. She leaned over the crime-
scene band of light, called to the reporter. They went into
a huddle.

David grimaced. Whatever the ultimate headline, it
would probably involve Annie Trey, and was not likely to
do her any good. The band of light played across Angie
Nassif's waistline. Later, when everyone was gone, that
band of light would give out a bone-rattling shock to
anyone trying to cross into the crime scene. Too early now.
Too bad.

Behind them, the door to the police van opened from the
side, and an Elaki rolled down the ramp, sliding sideways
on his bottom fringe.

String. His alien partner.

The Elaki had come to Earth with attitude—patronizing,
fascinated, slightly repelled. They were way ahead in the
social sciences and shared their knowledge freely. If some
speculated that their generosity was motivated by the op-
portunity to use humans as objects to further their studies,
so be it. The benefits were many—a cure for schizophrenia

and manic depression, to name two. Elaki were openly racist; people were inferior and smelled offensively of strong cheese, yet Elaki doctors were more compassionate than human ones, and Elaki excelled in law enforcement as well as in crime.

They also brewed a mean cup of coffee.

They were, on the average, seven feet tall, dark on the back and sides, pink to ivory on the tender belly. Their eyes protruded from stalks, and they moved with a peculiar rolling motion on a set of muscles beneath a scaled, iridescent fringe. They were thin, no ballast, and would blow away in a strong wind, constructed very much like an upright stingray. They smelled faintly of freshly cut limes. Intelligent usually, ever curious, and always judgmental.

String was not a particularly handsome specimen—he had bare patches where the scales had fallen away and not grown back. Elaki scars, David decided. His left eye prong drooped and his colors had faded, as if he'd been one too many times through a hot-water wash.

David saw String's eyestalk twitch. The Elaki was nervous; David could tell from the side-to-side jitter that reminded him of a little kid who has to go to the bathroom. String swiveled an eye prong and caught sight of him coming up the exit ramp.

"Ah. Detective David." The Elaki turned his back on the crime-scene band and scurrying humans, and focused his attention on the bottom of the ramp. Elaki-Town. "This must wrap around to be quick and gone."

David gave the Elaki a half-smile, meaningless to an alien. "Do you mean wrap things up?"

String turned slowly, his back to the bottom of the ramp. "Much is the menace, Detective David. Do you not feel it?"

Actually, he did. "Elaki-Town?"

String waved a fin. "Where would the light be if not on? Why the congregation?"

"Elaki on the sidewalks. That's unusual?"

"But yessss."

David felt the hair stir on the back of his neck. String

was afraid. String was never afraid.

The Elaki moved close to David, almost touching, voice low. "Most unusual, the behavior this. I ask you, if is just to be the gawking of, why not closer, where they can see?"

"They'd have to turn their backs if they came close. Elaki etiquette."

String cocked an eye prong. "That is the politeness, Detective David."

"If they keep their distance, can they look?"

"This is not so, Detective David. There are many Elaki, hidden down in darkness, all but to watch. And in such a place. These are not the best elements Elaki here, surely you know this."

David frowned. "How bad, String?"

"Remember hate crime riots, and fire bombs?"

David raised an eyebrow. "That bad?"

"Potential worse if it goes," String said. "This is not to be the kid."

"The kid?"

"I am not to joke you."

"Okay." David tried to look everywhere at once, caught sight of Angie Nassif and the media man. The camera was out, a recorder going. He looked at String. "Where's Mel?"

The Elaki grew still. "Have spoken to Halliday, Captain. Mel messaged first. Should be on the route."

David nodded. "Get with the techs and see how long before they can wrap. Push everybody but the holographer—if we have to leave in a hurry that may be all we'll have to fall back on."

String waved a fin. Assent. Holograms made good casebooks for presentation in court.

David looked over his shoulder at Elaki-Town, bit his lip. There was movement on the sidewalks, where before it had been still. Tension made his stomach tight. He wondered where Mel was. Decided he couldn't leave with his partner enroute and possibly arriving alone to face who knew what. He crooked a finger at the uniform who had taken his arm in the weeds.

"Two things, and quickly. Get the comm tech to see if he can get voice contact with Detective Mel Burnett, Homicide. And then I want you—and you personally, you understand?"

The boy nodded, and David saw a film of sweat on his upper lip. He looked closer. Not sweat. A thin attempt at a mustache.

Hiring before they could grow facial hair? Something very disturbing about that. He looked around, wondering if he was the only grown-up. He had a strong feeling of responsibility to all these young faces, and he wanted everybody out.

He heard bells, suddenly, distant but distinct. He looked at String, saw the Elaki freeze, twitch, and swivel an eyestalk his way. They'd been partners a while now. David knew, without asking, that the sound of bells was not a good thing, and that it was high time to haul ass.

String scurried to the CSU van and David turned back to the uniform. "Get a car and drive Ms. Trey and her baby home."

The boy's eyes widened, and he nodded.

"I didn't catch your name," David said, squinting at the shoulder tag.

"Alec Arnold. Patrolman Arnold."

David nodded. "I would consider it a personal favor, Patrolman Arnold, as well as a good sign of your professionalism, if you show Ms. Trey the utmost courtesy."

The patrolman's eyes went tight.

David frowned. "Is that a problem for you?"

"No sir, it's not a problem for me."

David looked at the boy's blank face. "You're sure?"

Arnold nodded stiffly.

The bells rang again. No time.

"She won't hurt you," David said.

FIVE

THE TECHNICIAN WAITED WHILE DAVID WENT OVER THE trunk quickly, focused. The breeze carried the hint of rain-drops—nothing to two men who had spent the evening in a downpour. The CSU van was loaded, engine idling. String cocked an eye prong, swaying from side to side. Elaki impatience.

"See where it's torn through there?" The tech was a big guy, big nose, cleared his throat a lot.

New on the job, David decided. And nervous.

"You think whoever was trapped in the trunk of the car crawled through this hole here into the cab?"

The tech nodded. David frowned, trying to remember the man's name. Samuel Caper.

David looked at the dark opening, the jagged rent of fabric. "What did he use to open it up?"

The trunk was clean, except on one side where someone had spilled popcorn—a few weeks ago, from the look of it. No one carried tools in their cars these days. Not unless they were up to something.

David peered into the side pockets of the trunk. Luke Cochran had tools.

He looked up at the blue ball of light that wavered over his head. "Light lower please, and move to three o'clock."

The blue ball zipped sideways almost as the words were out of his mouth, giving the impression of an intelligent and underchallenged assistant.

Just a microchip, David reminded himself. He crooked a finger at Caper. "You looked at these?"

"Yes, sir. Waiting for the holographer to get them down."

David nodded. A shovel, almost new, bottom blade clumped with dried mud. David touched the dirt. Dry and

16

brittle; a tangle of dried brown root hanging loose. Blue plaid work gloves, also new, were tucked into the handle. Trowels.

"Everything's new," the technician said.

David gave the man a second look. He had a round baby face, stubbled with beard here in the middle of the night. His hair was razor cut and short, ears overlarge. Not a handsome man, but appealing, like a puppy.

"Good," David said.

The man's cheeks went pink. He had a big, sloppy grin that came from the heart.

"This is my first murder investigation, sir."

"David."

"What?"

"Call me David." David turned back to the trunk. "Doesn't look like he used the shovel to get through here; that dirt isn't disturbed. Check the trowels—"

"I'm not sure it was a he, sir."

David looked up. "Not a he?"

"Well, um, I know it would seem like the killers—"

"We don't have a body yet," David reminded him.

"No, sir. See, at first I thought Cochran had been put in the trunk, maybe, and tunneled into the car. But this Cochran was a big guy and that's a pretty small opening."

"Think birth canal." The voice was tired, and there was an edge.

David looked over his shoulder, saw his partner, Mel Burnett. Wondered how long he had been standing there. His suit was wrinkled and spotted with rain, shoes muddy. His brown, curly hair had gone wiry in the humidity.

"Where've you been?" David said.

Mel shrugged. "Out and about."

Something in Mel's voice made David give him a second look. "You okay?"

"Sure," Mel said, carefully offhand.

"Mel, this is Sam Caper. This is his first murder investigation."

Mel grinned, shook the man's hand, plastic gloves and all. "And us without a body."

Caper smiled like a cowed puppy.

"Mel won't hurt you," David said.

Mel looked at Caper. "You were saying?"

The technician blinked. His eyes were blue, bright and alert. "About the size of the person who crawled through that hole. I'm just guessing, but I don't think Cochran could have gotten through there."

Mel bent over and stuck his head in the trunk. He poked his hand through the hole. "Elaki might have made it through, but the sucker would have shed a million scales, and I don't see any. I got to say I agree with Sam here." Mel glanced up at David. "Whyn't you try and get your shoulders through there, David? Cochran's bigger than you, so—"

"I think it was a woman," Caper said.

David cocked his head. "Why? Could have been a small man."

"We, um, found a bracelet. An ankle bracelet, I think; it's bigger than the other kind."

Mel exchanged looks with David. "The other kind?"

Caper shifted his weight to one foot. "The wrist kind."

"You might have brought it up," David said mildly.

Mel grinned. "See, Sam, we don't mean to be irritable with you or nothing, but a real murder investigation's not like on TV where everybody gets together at the end and the hero brings out the surprise evidence. We don't have to bring people back after the commercial break, kiddo, so we try to share the evidence as it comes up. Especially since we're all kind of standing around in the rain. Being human." Mel glanced at String, standing next to the driver's window of the CSU van. "Some of us, anyway."

Caper lifted his chin. "My fault. It's sealed up, they've got it in the van. Want to see it?"

"Sure," Mel said.

David shook his head. "No. Let's clear out. The tow truck—" He heard a shout, looked up. "Good. It's here. We need to get the car and everybody out of here."

Mel raised an eyebrow. "What's your hurry, David? I just got here. You interviewed the car yet?"

The tow truck pulled up, and the driver leaned out the window. "Okay if we set the program and let it go in under its own speed?"

David took a deep breath. "*No*. Put it on your flatbed, I don't want it out on the road. Evidence, and we're still looking at it."

"They told me at Dispatch it was a rush."

"It is a rush. But put it on your flatbed."

"Yessiree, boss."

David grimaced.

"Should I take the tools?" Caper asked.

Time, David thought. Caper would have bags. Labels. He realized he hadn't heard the bells in a while. Was that good or bad? He looked at String. Hard to tell.

"Pack up and go?" Caper asked.

"Yes."

Caper stuck his hands in his pockets. "Come on, Leon."

The light zipped out of the trunk, whizzing close to David's cheek. Caper headed for the CSU van, light bobbing obediently behind.

"Now ain't that sweet?" Mel said.

David looked at him. "Leon?"

Mel shrugged. "So what's the rush here? You worried the rain's gonna start back up?"

"Hey, Mel, you think I could get any wetter?"

"Now that you mention it, no."

"Elaki-Town," David said.

The tow truck operator headed for the car, and David and Mel moved away, huddled close up into the tree line.

Mel took a breath, waved a hand toward the town. "It looks weird down there. Dark. Something going on?"

"I don't know. String said—"

"Something obtuse, no doubt."

David nodded, stuck his hands in his pockets. The scrape on the back of his hand stung, started oozing blood. "Where were you tonight?"

Mel hunched his shoulders. Rolled his eyes. "You sound like my mother." He said it lightly. Always a joke.

David waited.

"David, I'm getting worried about Miriam. Damn worried, you want to know the truth."

"You seen her since your last fight?"

"*Last* fight? You make us sound like contenders. Considering you and Rose—"

"We aren't. Considering me and Rose. Answer the question."

"Yes sir, Officer. The answer is no. I haven't seen her or talked to her. And neither has anybody else."

David frowned, looked at Mel carefully. Even in the dim street light he could see Mel's face was drawn, pale beneath his tan, eyes dark, smudged, exhausted.

"No one?"

"No one I can find, and I been looking. She hasn't been in the lab, won't answer the phone, missed the last two classes she was supposed to teach."

David felt odd, prickly, the old cop instinct revving, a call to arms. "Talked to her sister?"

Mel swallowed, voice rough. "No. Can't get her on the phone."

It seemed the obvious move, but David did not comment. "You been inside her place?"

"No."

"No?"

"Didn't sit right. All her appliances are there watching, keeping records. If she passed out or something, they'd call for help. So if I go in there, after we had a fight, it's like an invasion. But it's been long enough, so I'm going. That's why I'm here, to get you to go with me. Make it official. I'm the boyfriend, after all. Suspect number one."

"Okay. Send your car home, we'll ride together. And, Mel?"

"Yeah?"

"Don't leave town."

"Nice to know somebody's still got a sense of humor."

SIX

DAVID AND MEL WERE SITTING IN THE DARK, WHISPERING, David's car pulled off the ramp and out of the way. The CSU van had just pulled out. A groan of metal, and the tow truck driver was done, black Visck gleaming on the flatbed. A patrol officer stayed in his car, waiting to provide escort.

The crumpled front end of the Visck made David wince. It was a beautiful car.

Mel drummed his fingers on the armrest. "Okay now, big Daddy? Everybody's gone, all right and tight. Can we leave now?"

It would be irresponsible to leave some poor schmuck in uniform alone here in the dark this close to Elaki-Town, even on a normal night. David gave Mel a look.

Nothing to see in the dark.

David started the car, called up the headlights. He programmed the navigator, but the car did not engage the tracks.

"You ever clean this car?" Mel kicked at something on the floor. "What is this, anyway? You been carting your kids around?"

David leaned over the console and picked the teddy bear up. Must belong to little Jenny Trey. David thought of the tiny girl, face flushed and feverish. Could she fall asleep without the bear? At that age, Kendra, his oldest, had a stuffed purple and green snake she carried everywhere, including to bed. Try to settle her in without it, and there'd be hell to pay.

David settled the bear in his lap. His hand was bloody, and he held the bear carefully, trying not to soil it.

"That yours, is it? Cause I have a blanket myself."

"Funny, Mel. I wonder why we aren't moving."

21

"Close proximity," the car said.

David looked at Mel. "What?"

"Somebody standing by the car, Detective David Silver. Moving ahead would put subject in danger."

David put a hand on the door.

Mel grabbed his arm, knocking the bear sideways. "*Wait* a minute. This car's armored and we're not. Want to exercise just a little—"

David grabbed the bear absently, wiped fog from the window and squinted. An Elaki, backside view.

"It's just String."

"You sure, David? Look for that fishhook scar on the right side."

"Too dark," David said.

"Then how you know it's him?"

"He slouches."

"Damn. Now that you come to mention it, String's the only Elaki I ever seen with bad posture."

David opened the car door. "String? *String?*"

The Elaki turned. "Ssssh, Detective David. Am listening."

"What for am listening?" Mel asked.

String swiveled. "For the bells."

"I don't hear any bells," Mel said.

"Not good this," String said. "Bells have stopped. Must the go now."

David reached backward, opened the door to the back seat. "Help a lot if you got in."

The Elaki surged toward the car, then skidded to a halt. "Take van."

"Ah, *Jesus*," Mel said. "We going to shuffle cars all night? We're already in here, String. Don't go balky. We rode in the van last time. I don't like hanging onto them straps, and you take the corners so fast, I about get a concussion."

String went headfirst into the back, muttering.

"Did you say 'hernia'?" Mel asked. " 'Cause Elaki don't get hernias." He looked at David. "Do they?"

String hissed. "Isss translation, very like this hernia,

folding fringe, *most* uncomfortable.''

''Close the door and close your yap.''

''And how this to accomplish, the yap closing? Bottom scale gymnastics bizarre?''

Mel looked at David. ''I think what he means is he can't reach the door handle.''

David nodded, got out, tucked String's bottom fringe away from the edge of the door. Scales dropped, falling into the crack. David shut the door gently, then stopped, driver's door open, dome light bright—the only light visible except for the Interstate.

What was it he had heard?

The noise came again, a sort of whistle, but not quite—a noise made by something alive, but nothing David had ever heard. The whistle sounded again, followed by a trilling coo.

''What the hell was that?'' Mel said.

''Sound too much like the trillopy,'' String said.

''What's trillopy, some musical instrument?''

The Elaki's voice sounded hollow, coming from the back seat, and David wondered if String was catching a cold.

''Trillopy is predator hunting animal. Only found home planet, most to be relieved. Completely illegal Earth residence. Not indigenous here.''

''What do you *mean* by all of that?'' Mel said. ''David, will you get in the car? Do I have to beg here?''

David got in the driver's seat, then looked back at String. ''He's worried about Miriam. She's missing, and they had a fight.''

''Most worrisome. What fight about?''

''Can we go now, Detective David Silver?''

David frowned at the car. ''Go already.''

''Toilet seats,'' Mel said.

''Who goes first in contention?'' String asked.

The car inched forward, caught the tracks, increased speed. David steered, looked from side to side to make sure no one was left behind.

Mel snapped his seat belt. ''*No*, not who goes first; that would be stupid.''

"What, then?" String said.

Mel muttered something under his breath.

"What was that?" David asked.

"I just asked her not to slam the lid. It was no big—"

"You on the seat when lid be slammed?"

"*No*, I wasn't on the . . . String, there are some things that aren't going to make sense to you 'cause you're not human, you're Elaki. You're *alien*."

"No need to be sorry, Detective Mel. Unless sorry are you human."

David rubbed the back of his neck. "Children, please."

Mel looked out the window. "David, this goddamn car missed the exit. Miriam's apartment is at the university—"

"I am following navigational instruction to the letter," the car said.

"We're going to Annie Trey's."

String and Mel went silent.

"Yes," David said. "*The* Annie Trey. I'll fill you in on the way."

"Kind of late to be questioning her," Mel said.

David held up the teddy bear. "We're on a mission of mercy."

SEVEN

DAVID TUCKED THE TEDDY BEAR INTO THE CROOK OF HIS arm.

Mel pointed a finger. "Don't get too attached to that little guy; he don't belong to you."

David grinned. It was an old bear, this teddy. He had never seen one quite like it. At twenty-eight inches tall, it was almost as big as little Jenny. It had a ribbon around its neck, a sweet, solemn face. Big head, long nose, short feet, and long arms. Its fur was soft, almost silky, well-loved. A clump of dried egg yolk adorned the back of one ear.

David wondered where Annie Trey had picked it up, thinking he would like one for Mattie. The bear had the aged air that said "Goodwill." Best not to ask.

The car ran ragged as they approached Annie Trey's neighborhood. The road rails were old here, poorly maintained. Connemara was the neighborhood label in the navigational program, but the area was known around town as Cracker Village. It was bad—largely populated by dirt-poor Southerners, and rounded out by enclaves of cultural diehards from the Midwest, Jersey, and Saigon. The Vietnamese and the Southerners cooked and ran the clubs, the Jerseyites ran the garages and digital shops, and the Midwesterners were there to disapprove. The Texans were a world unto themselves. Most people hoped they'd keep it that way.

The first grid of Cracker Village was jammed with shotgun houses, barely a handsbreath between sagging roofs. The buildings were over a hundred years old—antique firetraps, shoddy and dangerous, and superior to the street of tenements where Annie Trey lived.

The car tires bumped over a retreaded rail that rode like

gravel. String shifted in the back seat. "This is the unnecessary roughness."

Mel rubbed the tip of his nose. "Be lucky if we don't blow a tire."

The car took them to an empty parking lot in back of a brick-and-mortar building. A peculiarity of the neighborhood. Parking lots—no cars. The pavement was littered with broken asphalt, dirt, snatches of old clothes. Thick yellow security lights made the pavement look somehow sweaty. The usual boxes of Jack Daniels and Coke provided a splash of color, and everywhere were piles of broken plates, ripped cushions, and old shoes—shoddy things no one wanted in a place where nobody had anything much.

Mel looked at David. "And I thought my apartment was a mess."

David got out of the car. "You two coming or not?"

"Sure as hell aren't staying in the parking lot."

"Car. Guard alert."

"No kidding, David Silver," the car said testily, born of a programmer with attitude. "Alert automatic in current location. Will report to precinct headquarters if not checked back within the hour."

David nodded. He realized the car couldn't see him, but it didn't need an answer. It certainly didn't deserve one.

Aliens were an oddity in this part of the city. David and Mel kept String between them.

Clumps of people milled under the overhang in front of the building. It was late—wet and steamy enough that people talked slowly, even for Southerners, and moved even less. The city had run out of money for subsidized air conditioning, and the apartments, cubbies built with central air in mind, were breathless by late spring. On these long August nights, residents were forced out of their homes by the heat.

Tonight most people were inside, driven there by the rain.

A woman moved sideways on the front stoop to let them through. Her breasts were loose and large under a sleeveless sweater, and she had bad teeth, and the pronounced jaw and receding chin that bespoke generations of poverty. David wondered if the deep South was so bad that Cracker Village was an improvement, or if the people here were too tired or broke to go home.

Just another place, he figured. No better, maybe worse; just different.

A street light flickered out. The humidity made halos around the handful that worked. David expected an aura of animosity, but got apathy instead. The rain had turned people desultory.

"Hey."

David tensed. There were only three of them.

"Hey, Elaki-sir. What's yer name, fella?"

String drifted sideways, eye prong cocked.

Mel shook his head. "Ignore 'em, String."

"But polite they be, says 'sir.' "

"That's Southern heckling, Gumby. They'll 'sir' you before they spit on your foot."

"Spit?"

"Just a form of speech."

"Will not tolerate this *spit*."

"String, go in, will you?"

The inside foyer was a checkerboard black-and-white linoleum, streaked wet and grey with grunge. Mel slipped, caught himself, muttered under his breath.

He ran a finger under the collar of his shirt. "Can't hardly breathe in here."

The foyer narrowed into a hallway, close and claustrophobic enough to make David's chest go tight. The floor was covered in worn wood plank, and David stepped carefully, avoiding a dark stain of something he didn't care to know better. The wall on the right was old brick and had been painted white, sometime before his first child was born. The other side of the wall was the porous yellow plasticine that lasted forever, like all things ugly.

Another small form of hell, David thought, rounding a corner. He looked up. "Stairs."

Mel looked relieved. "I was beginning to wonder. What's her number?"

"Three-oh-two."

The stairs clanged underfoot, a surprise since they looked like wood. David took a second look. Metal, painted over to look like wood. Odd this, but nicely done. String zigged and zagged at the foot of the staircase.

"David?"

"Yeah, Mel?"

"Better give our buddy here a lift."

"This is not to be the necessaries."

David stepped backward, to String's left, while Mel took the right side.

"One . . . two . . . three . . ." David felt a fin slip, and String emitted a sharp whistle and slid sideways.

"Dignified this cannot be," String said.

Mel groaned. "My back don't like it either, but we don't got all night while you skitter back and forth in the hallway there, and it ain't safe to leave you alone."

"I do not do this 'scatter.' "

"The hell you don't."

"The hell, then."

"David, did you hear that? This Elaki's learning to cuss."

David felt sweat trickle down his back, and he wished he had a hand free to wipe his forehead. He thought about showers and icy beer.

A child wailed as they turned the corner. David and Mel set String down gently. A welcoming committee awaited, outside in the hallway at the top of the stairs.

EIGHT

THE MAN WHO SAT ON THE TOP STEPS BLOCKING THEIR way was in his thirties or forties, hair dark blond with red highlights. His eyebrows were startling—thick white crescents. He had a big nose and the sun-wrinkled face of a man who earns his living outdoors. His forearms, bare and hairy, were muscular. He reminded David of Popeye.

David looked into his eyes and saw a child.

He wore cheap blue workpants, heavy brown work shoes, a short-sleeved mustard-yellow shirt that made David wonder who dressed him every morning. But he was smiling in that open, friendly way David associated with the mentally handicapped, and he laughed when he caught sight of String.

"See that, Val? That's an Elaki, isn't he?"

"Yeah, Eddie, that's an Elaki." A woman stood at the top of the stairs beside a very old man—making a committee of three. She did not look friendly. The old man looked worried. Somewhere behind them, behind closed doors, a child sobbed, weary and choked.

"Who might you be?" the woman said, in a low, steady voice that caught David's attention.

"Who's asking," Mel said. He wiped sweat from the back of his neck.

The woman tilted her head sideways and considered him. She had beautiful skin, David thought, blue-black and glowing with sweat in the impossible heat of the building. She was barefooted, wearing a white cotton dress that was shaped by the curve of her small breasts, narrow hips, and the sweet, gentle swell of her belly. Her hair was up off her neck, casually pinned up in the way some women have of twisting their hair this way and that to get it out of their way, achieving a casual sexiness in seconds that other women cannot achieve in hours of primping. Her eyes were dark brown, almost black, her face somehow missing pretty but achieving handsome.

It was a serious face, and she wasn't smiling. She was looking at Mel with her long neck arched. "*I'm* asking. And I know who *I* am. Who I am is not the issue. I'm wanting to know who you are, and you got one minute to tell me before I call the police."

"They'll come, too." This from the old man, a brittle ancient whose tone of voice was querulous and unconvincing. "I have friends on the force, and a nephew in the IRS."

David looked at the old man, knowing there would be no friends on the force, no nephew in the IRS.

"We *are* the police," Mel said.

David offered his ID.

It took the sass out of them, if not the wariness. David did not know whether to laugh or cry, watching them deflate, exchange looks, regroup.

Still the enemy, he thought, just a different flavor.

"We don't know nuthin about nuthin." Eddie's wide smile belied the challenge of his words. The old man patted him on the shoulder with a hand that trembled.

"I'm Detective David Silver," David said. None of them had given his ID a second glance. They were the kind of people who knew cops when they saw them. "And you are?"

"I'm Mr. Dandy." If the old man had a first name, he didn't admit to it.

His striped shirt was spotless, but worn thin with frayed cuffs, and buttoned tightly at the wrist and the long, thin neck. He wore a blue-and-white tie, cuffed khaki pants that hung loose on a frame nearly skeletal, and brown leather suspenders that David guessed he wore every day of his life. His ears stuck out. His hair was short on the sides, thick at top, white and healthy and parted on one side. He was bony and tall, all joints and long, thin fingers.

"I'm Eddie Eyebrows," the man on the steps said. He offered David a hand, grinned at the Elaki, waved.

David liked the way he said 'eyebrows,' as if it was the name he'd been born with. He had pulled the sting out of what was likely a constant taunt by taking ownership.

"Valentine," the woman said.

"Just Valentine?" David asked.

"All *you* need to know. You here for Annie?"

David did not like the feeling he got here. He did not want to play the heavy with these people.

"We're just here to ask her some questions." Why, he asked himself, did he feel the need to earn this woman's approval?

Valentine folded her arms. "This time of night? When she's got a sick baby on her hands?"

David held up the teddy. "I've got the bear."

Eddie leaped up and clapped his hands. "He's got it, Val; it's the bear, Jenny's bear!"

The transformation was instantaneous and beautiful, smiles all around.

"My hero," Mel muttered.

Mr. Dandy held out a hand. "Right this way, good sir. I know one little girlie who's going to be glad to see you."

Valentine folded her arms, nodded at David. "Just be sure you leave that door open when you have your little talk."

Mel waved a hand. "Yeah, Your Highness, whatever. Bring on the bear, will you, David, and let's get on with this."

NINE

ALL OF DAVID'S CHILDREN HAD LOVED A SPECIAL CUDDLY
when they were toddlers—Kendra's had been a stuffed
snake, Lisa had a Winnie the Pooh, and Mattie had only
recently given up custody of a blanket named Pid. Trying
to get one of them to sleep without their special toy was
always a crisis—the kind of crisis Annie Trey was having
with Jenny.

Her apartment was known as a junior—two rooms,
L-shaped, with a tiny kitchen attached to a living room, and
a closet-sized bedroom off one side. She did not have very
many things; a battered rocker with an old green cushion,
a cubed plastic love seat—dirt-cheap even brand new. A
wire lamp. Large-screen TV tacked to one wall.

Everything that she had evidently wanted in the way of
furniture was painted on the walls. Mel turned a circle,
studying. He pointed a finger at Annie Trey.

"You the artist?"

She jiggled the baby. Looked at Mel a long moment, then
shrugged. "Yeah."

Her taste ran to the simple—chunky lines of Scandina-
vian furniture, blond wood, boxy silhouettes. There was a
couch on one side, with end tables. The other side showed
shelves that held a complicated sound system, a computer,
stacks of laser discs. Another wall showed an entertainment
center and a grandfather clock.

Annie Trey paced the room, bouncing Jenny up and
down in her arms. "*Hush*, honey." The baby clutched the
teddy bear and burrowed her head in Annie's shoulder, sob-
bing as if her heart would break. Annie looked at David,
but didn't really see him. She ran a hand through her hair.
"I'm sorry, we'll just have to talk while she cries, 'less you

want to wait on this. I thought the bear would turn the trick.''

String looked at David. ''She is the artist of the stairs.''

He nodded. It was the outside wall that drew him.

She had painted a large bay window, where the architect had committed the sin of not having one. Curtains billowed, framing a view of a river, tug boat moving in the ripples. David walked across the room, drawn by the glint of sunlight on water. It was good. Very good. Almost, he had been fooled.

A hole had been punched through the yellow plasticine beneath the window—all the way through the mortar to the outside. It was a small opening, no more than three inches across and two inches high. A small piece of white lace was tacked across the top—the closest Annie Trey came to a real window.

David felt tired. It was the little things people did that sometimes broke his heart.

''Maybe we should come back at a better time,'' Mel said.

String slid sideways toward the baby. ''But what of the pouchling? We cannot just leave to the tears.'' He moved back and forth on his bottom fringe. ''Is this pouchling in need of nourishment?''

Annie patted the baby's back. ''I tried to give her a bottle just a minute ago, and she throw'd it acrost the room. Come on, sweetie, come on, baby. Hush now. Got Fuzzy Bear, see?''

Jenny closed her eyes and the sobs stopped. She hiccupped, then made a little snore. David and Mel took a deep breath.

Annie held a finger to her lips and headed for the bedroom. The baby woke up coughing before she made it across the room.

Mel looked at David. ''Let's go and leave this woman in peace.''

String waved a fin. ''There is not the peace here, Detective Mel.''

''Yeah, but—''

Annie Trey had tears in her eyes. "Please, Jenny. Hush, baby."

David wondered how she'd made it with two. One of them died, he reminded himself.

He held out his arms. "You mind?"

She handed him the baby but hovered close, waiting to snatch her back. "She's a good baby, she's just feeling real bad."

"She had cough medicine in a while?" David asked.

Annie nodded. "Don't get another dose for at least two hours."

David settled into the rocking chair. Jenny twisted sideways, whimpered. He tucked Fuzzy Bear into the crook of his arm and the little girl laid her head wearily on the bear's tummy. David took the thin cotton blanket tangled in the chubby little legs and put it on top of the child's head, covering both temples.

"You forget which end is up?" Mel said.

David began to rock gently. Jenny watched him, heavy-eyed and cautious. He smiled at her, rocking. The child snuggled deeper into his arms. The coughing stopped. The baby's eyes closed. She hiccupped twice, and was asleep.

"Experienced father," Mel said.

Annie gave David a wary half smile.

"Isss the magic touch," from String.

David shrugged. It was a trick he had learned from his father, a trick that always worked with his girls when they were coughing and could not sleep. He stood up and headed for the bedroom. The room was tiny and held a white crib, a wicker changing table, and an empty bassinet.

A mobile had been painted on the wall over the crib. One had been started by the bassinet, then left unfinished. A new picture had been painted where the mobile left off. Smaller, darker, fresh paint.

David settled the child into the crib, keeping the blanket over her head and off her face. He tucked the bear in next to her. The picture caught his attention again, held him.

It showed a huge tree, old, decaying, flanked by smaller, younger trees, leaves turquoise under white light. An orange, red-tinged flame leapt up the center of the tree, crisping the edges of the bark, shattering the serenity of the forest.

David heard a noise, saw Annie Trey standing in the doorway, watching him. She went behind him to the crib, shifting the blanket to her own specifications—typical mother, that. She herded him out, motioning for him to reclaim the rocking chair, while she sat cross-legged on the floor.

She settled heavily, shoulders drooping. "What was it y'all wanted to know?"

David felt guilty, keeping this child-mother up. "I'd like you to tell me everything you remember about the night Luke Cochran disappeared."

Annie Trey nodded and chewed her lip.

David watched her with pain and pleasure, thinking she reminded him of Teddy. Not in looks—Teddy was pretty and wise, her voice pitched low but full of fun. And Teddy had an aura of energy, like a puppy—you never expected her to sit still. Annie Trey was exhausted, perfectly willing to sit if she had the chance. She moved differently, slower, almost hesitantly.

David had not spoken to Teddy in months. Best not. Hearing her voice would eat up the distance he was barely managing, leaving him raw again, starting from scratch.

But they were both from the South, Teddy and Annie Trey, and there was more to their similarity than the accent. Maybe it was the air they both had of having their backs to the wall.

Mel settled back against the couch, eyes half closed. "Sure you're up for this?" he asked.

Annie nodded, chin sharp. She drew her legs up, elbows on knees.

"Go back to the night you made the call, the night Luke disappeared. Start at the beginning. What were you doing?"

"I was drinking iced tea. It was real hot, real humid. And Jenny had just started in with this cold, been up and fussy all day, wouldn't go down for her nap. I was supposed to meet Luke and that forensic lady. Ms. Miriam Kellog.''

David turned and looked at Mel, who was nodding. Miriam? Mel did not seem surprised.

"Why were you meeting Miriam?"

Annie looked at the floor. David slid forward in the rocking chair, and it tipped forward as he strained to catch Annie's soft monotone.

"She was doing a . . . tests, and all of that. On my baby, Hank."

David had not heard the baby's name before. It made the child seem more real, and he thought of the empty bassinet in the nursery, by Jenny's little white crib.

Annie's chin drooped to her chest. "They still don't know what he died of."

All of that, David thought, trying not to imagine the autopsy of an infant.

"She told me even if she couldn't find out for definite, if it was a virus or a bacteria germ, she could at least make sure people knew it wasn't me that did it. It wasn't poison, or nothing like that." Annie looked up at David. "She was real nice to me. We talked a lot about what might have made Hank sick, and she ran them people over at the hospital pretty hard."

String moved sideways, shedding scales. "What hospital will this be?"

Annie looked at the Elaki as if she were surprised he could talk. "University Hospital, Meridian Branch. For indigents; you know the one."

David rubbed his thumb. "Are you saying that Miriam was going to meet Luke the night he disappeared?"

Annie nodded. "We was all supposed to meet, but the baby was sick, so I couldn't go."

"Did Miriam go?"

She shrugged. "I left a message on her machine before I called Luke. I didn't hear from her but I figured she got it."

"You haven't heard from Miriam since Luke disappeared?"

"No, sir, I haven't."

David took a quick look at Mel, saw the lines of weariness and worry, the sag of his shoulders. Making the same connections, most likely. He thought about Caper's suggestion that it was a woman who had been locked in the trunk of Cochran's car. Maybe this was not Luke Cochran in the wrong place at the wrong time, snagged by Mr. Stranger Danger. Maybe this was something else. Had Cochran or Miriam been targeted? Cochran had been picked up at his dorm room, so he was the likely target. Maybe Miriam was the one in the wrong place at the wrong time.

"Tell us about the phone call," Mel said.

David figured that no one who didn't know Mel very well would pick up that tremor in his voice.

Annie closed her eyes. "Luke was in his room when I called. I told him Jen was sick, and he . . . he asked about if it was serious. I said no, just a cold, but that she had just got to sleep, and could maybe they come here? And he said maybe we should do it some other night. But I said no, we had to hurry things up, or they might take Jenny from me. So then I ask him something, but he doesn't seem like he's listening. And suddenly he yells. He says, like, 'Hey, what are they'—" She looked at String, turned red. " 'Them *folks* doing with my car?' Then he goes, 'Hang on, be right back.' And that was it."

David cocked his head. "Folks? He didn't really say 'folks,' did he?"

Annie shifted sideways in her chair, avoided looking at String. "He said 'frigging bellybrains,' but I didn't want to say that in front of him."

"The offensive will not take further," String said.

"So it was Elaki down there, messing with the car." Mel scratched his chin. "That it? He say anything else?"

"That was his last words to me."

Mel leaned forward. "And Miriam hasn't been in touch?"

Annie glanced down at the floor. "No, sir."

"You don't think it's odd, her not calling?" Mel asked. "I mean, with you worried about your babies and all?"

"I figure she's been taking care of things. And, if you got to know, I been kind of afraid to stir things up."

TEN

THERE WAS ANOTHER WELCOMING COMMITTEE, PARTY OF one, waiting on the landing as they came out of Annie Trey's apartment. The little girl tapped a small bare foot. She did not look happy.

Mel looked down at her and waved. She scowled. She wore a thin cotton nightgown that hung just below her knees, stark white against smooth, baby-fine black skin. Her hair was long and thick, her eyes brown, the whites so white they were almost blue. She clutched a black kitten in one arm. The kitten was a long-hair, with round blue eyes and one white paw.

Mel grinned at her snub. "Why the frownie face, kiddo?"

"My name is'n kiddo, is Cassidy."

"Your mama know you're out here?"

"My Mama is Valentine. She midwifes babies wif her own two hands. That means helping them come out of their mama. And she sings Italian in the Dixie-Saigon Club. She sings church music too, but that's just on Sunday. When I grow up, I'm going to sing. Mama says I have a pretty voice, if I could learn to carry a tune."

"But does she know you're out here?"

"She's tired and dead asleep, 'cause my mama works hard, so I stood up on a chair and undid the locks." She squinched her eyes. "You-all are the mens come to take Jenny away from Annie. I'm not going to let you." The girl stood stiff-legged and afraid, and David had never felt so much the villain. "Annie is a good mama and nice to me, and when I get bigger I'm going to be Jen's baby-sitter."

"We're not here to take Jenny," David said.

"That's what they all say."

David looked at Mel and hid a smile. An old line, but the world-weary delivery was priceless.

"What's your kitty's name?" David asked.

"Baby Blue. He's two months old. He almost died."

Mel raised an eyebrow. "That so?"

"I found him in the road. He was so little, he could fit right in my mama's hand."

David glanced at Cassidy's own hand, the tiny fingers buried in the cat's fur.

"He was sick and wouldn't eat. So Annie mix some milk and sugar and dipped her finger on it and he lick it off. And then he felt better after a while and drank it all up. So you got to be nice to Annie. Mama said you wouldn't leave that door open and you were probably up to no good like most mens she know."

"The door was closed because we're police officers and we had private business."

String surged forward. "Time for pouchling to go back inside, to be sleeping times."

The cat hissed, fur going thick, and String backed away. Cats and Elaki never mixed.

David jerked a thumb toward the door to Valentine's apartment. "I'm going to wait out here till you're inside, and I hear you lock the door."

"Will Annie be okay?" The little girl gave David a look that would melt sterner stuff than he was made of.

"Annie will be okay."

The kitten was squirming. David opened the door to Valentine's apartment—simple door, simple lock, no voice-activated alarms or recognition systems for the people who needed them most.

"Good night, little pouchling," String said.

"Good night, sir."

The door closed softly. Mel and String headed down the stairs, while David stayed and listened for the lock.

ELEVEN

THE CARS HAD BALKED AT MEETING THEM IN CRACKER Village, some regulation or another, so they'd congregated outside of Stella's Deli on Marsh and Third. The deli was closed, the street dark, car headlights reflecting in the safety glass of the storefront, arcing across brick walls.

David leaned against the car door, arms folded. "It's late, Mel, and you look like hell."

"Don't be sweet-talking me, David."

String made a moaning sound as he slithered from the back seat of the car onto the pavement.

David shrugged. "Look, if you want to go to Miriam's tonight, we'll go right now. It's just we're both tired and—"

"You're afraid we'll, like, miss a clue?"

"Might be better to go tomorrow, after we've had some sleep."

String was upright again, making a whistling noise through the oxygen slits on his belly. The slits formed a perpetual happy face on his tender, inner pink hide.

"Isss most stupid, this lack of the van."

Mel looked at him. "Yeah, but String, we'd like to get there in one piece, and with you driving, that's not guaranteed."

"For this I have the cricked fringe-scale?"

"How long since you talked to her?" David asked.

"Night before this Cochran kid disappeared. That was Miriam in that kid's trunk—you caught that, did you?"

David looked at the sidewalk. "Very possible."

"This Cochran disappears at same of the time isss Miriam Kellog, sleep partner of Detective Mel."

" 'Sleep partner,' String? Call her my girlfriend, okay?"

"Isss okay. This Miriam sleep . . . girl partner—"

41

"Girl*friend*."

"But I wish to imply the romantic."

"Girlfriend does imply the romantic."

"Then if you are the man friend of myssself and Detective David—"

"That's different."

"In some cases I understand—"

"*String*, for God's sake—"

David held up a hand. "Miriam did the autopsy on the Trey baby, and Cochran goes missing the same night he's supposed to meet Miriam and Annie. Miriam hasn't been seen or heard from since. Of course it's connected. Mel, you checked her office, and with her sister, right?"

"Her sister won't take my calls. And Miriam's on leave of absence, doing research at the university, advising some of the doctoral candidates. So nobody's keeping track of her."

"Except you," David said.

"And I can't find her."

"You don't think she's staying away because she's mad?"

"She might stay away from me, but not her apartment, not her work. I want a look at that ankle bracelet that tech found."

"Think you'd recognize it?" David asked.

Mel shrugged. "I got stuff in my drawers at home I don't recognize."

String teetered back and forth on his bottom fringe. "Pouchling isss mine for two-day session. If wish to go here now to the place of the Miriam Kellog, must call chemaki and arrange the makings."

David wished he had a grouping of five adults he could call on for help with the care of *his* offspring. Of course, even with Elaki, the brunt of pouchling care fell on the Mother-One. Some things never changed.

"Nah, String—David's right, I guess. Not much we can accomplish tonight."

String waved a fin and headed for his van. David opened his car door, got in. He looked at Mel, who was heading for his car, hands deep in his pockets. He stepped back out on the pavement, door hanging open.

"Detective David Silver, please close the door or the power pack—"

"Shut up," David said softly. "Mel?"

Mel turned, face in the shadows.

"Why don't you head home with me? Rose will behave if you're around, and you haven't seen the kids in ages."

Mel rubbed the back of his neck. "Need protection from my sister, huh?"

"Just lately she's been a little—"

"She find out about you and Teddy?"

David gave him a wary look. There was no hostility in Mel's face, just fatigue. "What about me and Teddy?"

"Yeah, right David, whatever you say." Mel shifted his weight. "I would like to see the kiddos."

Mel sent his car away. It pulled away from the curb, and he walked back quickly, settling with a sigh into the passenger's side of David's car. "You don't mind driving, do you?"

"No." David gave him a look. "How long have you known about Teddy?"

"David, I hate to bust your bubble, but you'd be hard put to find anybody in the department who doesn't know."

David opened his window to the steamy night breeze, turning the air conditioner on low. He felt the tires snug into the grid that led out of the city to his ten-acre farm.

"What's the problem between you and Miriam? Other than toilet seats, I mean."

Mel didn't answer. David looked sideways, saw his partner was asleep.

TWELVE

THE BUMP OF CAR TIRES GOING FROM GRID TO RAW PAVE-
ment brought David out of a sleepy daze. Mel did not wake
up. David dreaded this part of the drive when he was tired.
There was no grid on the two-lane rural road. The car could
go off the pavement and into the trees in a split second of
inattention. It was hard to imagine that less than thirty years
ago people had always driven this way. No wonder traffic
fatalities had been a major cause of death.

He had missed his father tonight when he returned the
teddy bear to little Jenny Trey. He always missed his dad
when he did something nice for kids.

That was one thing Teddy had given him—the answer
to his father's disappearance all those years ago. David always knew that his father was a good man, the kind of man
who would not abandon a ten-year-old boy and a manic-
depressive wife. Something had to have happened.

And something had.

Teddy was a psychic, working with the Saigo City Police
on a missing person case. David, who loathed psychics, had
loved and hated her from the very first day. The hate had
gone away. He wished the love would.

Teddy had found his father for him—dead all these
years, decomposing behind the wheel of his car, hidden
beneath the muddy brown waters of the Talmidge River.

The car had seen it all, reporting in after they'd pulled
it rusty and dripping from the water. A stupid killing in the
parking lot of a doughnut shop. His father had interfered,
earning a bullet, a quick death, and a hidden grave in dark,
muddy water.

An old, old crime, messy and violent and pointless, hap-
pening fast, as they usually did, causing pain that lasted a
lifetime.

David wondered how many times he had driven that Talmidge River Bridge while his father floated in the swift
dark waters, eyes blank and unseeing till they were eaten
by the fish.

Bad thoughts. *Let them go.*

For the first time in a long time, the farm looked good
to him when he pulled in the drive. He turned off the car
engine, waited for the headlights to dim.

He had an unexpected moment of happiness. Yes, the
house needed to be painted, and he did not have the time
to do it, or the money to pay someone else. And the leaves
of yet another baby dogwood tree were crispy and brown—
he could not make them grow. No doubt they resented
neglect.

The porch swing still hung crooked in spite of his best
efforts. The wind made it move, and he listened for the
familiar creak of rusty chain. The sky had lightened, easing
the weight of a bad night. It seemed like the nights were
always bad. Now was the best time, the time when the
darkness breathed easier, the world fresh and unsullied by
the day ahead. David stood in the driveway beside the car,
feeling the breeze against his hot skin.

And just like that, the happiness slipped away. He heard
a car engine on the road behind him, and saw that it was
running without lights, which could mean trouble, or nothing more than someone who had circumvented the safety
controls of a bossy automobile. People hated to be told
what to do.

The dark shape disappeared, engine noises fading. David
looked at Mel, saw he was awake and watchful. He wondered if it was the noise that had awakened him, or the
silence.

"What's up?" Mel said, voice sleep-shadowed and dull.
"We're home."

The dog barked as they came up the stairs.

"Duck," David said, and opened the door.

Mel went first into the living room, and bent down to
rub the dog's head. A wineglass arced from the hallway,

whizzed across the room, and smashed into the doorjamb
where his head had been.

The dog barked and whined and peed on the floor. Mel
looked at the shards of broken glass and the dark oval of
liquid on the carpet.

"Nothing like hanging out with the married folk, to
make a guy appreciate living alone."

The dog groaned and whimpered and rubbed against
David's shins in an intense, doggie ecstasy that made David
wonder if he oughtn't get home more often.

Rose had found the dog in a laboratory cage marked
DEAD MEAT, and when she was through trashing the lab,
she had taken pity on him and brought him home. She was
a freelance animal rights activist—the militant variety. David called the dog Meat, which annoyed the children, who
kept trying to call her Hildie.

"Rose throw something at you every time you come
home?" Mel asked.

David nodded.

"You tried to talk?"

"She won't."

"Hell, sooner or later, she's got to run out of dishes."
He raised his voice. "Hello, Rose!"

"Mel?" Rose came from the hallway into the living
room. As usual, she had left the lamp on low. Lately, David
had been wondering why she always left the light—Habit?
Welcome? Help with her aim?

Her hair was full and messy, thick dark hair, with a loose
natural wave. There were circles of fatigue under her eyes,
a swelling bruise on her cheekbone, a scrape on her chin.
She wore a loose black T-shirt that came to her thighs, and
thick white cotton socks.

New socks, David noticed, with a stab of something that
sort of felt like affection, and sort of felt like pain. Rose
would put on a new pair of socks every day, if they could
afford it. He pictured himself bringing her boxes of brand
new socks.

David, he thought, you romantic devil.

Rose gave Mel a hug. " 'Bout time you got out here to see me. You guys hungry?''

"What happened to your face?" Mel asked.

Rose touched the bruise. "Nothing."

"Yeah, well, it could be an improvement."

Rose yawned. "Come on in the kitchen; the girls and I had hamburger on a roll tonight, and we've got leftovers."

David trailed behind them, wondering if there would be anything else to eat. He had never understood their passion for hamburger on a roll.

"You want to warm it?" Rose asked.

Mel shook his head. "No way. We eat it cold."

David sat down at the small kitchen table. Rose rustled a package wrapped in butcher cling, put food on one of their few remaining plates, and set it in front of him. Then she and Mel stood side by side in front of the sink, munching happily, repeating some familiar ritual from their childhood. David wondered if Rose and the kids had happy rituals from which he was excluded. Rose took a single beer out of the refrigerator, opened the top and took a drink, then passed it among the three of them. David was grateful to be included. He preferred individual beers, and Rose liked to share—another point of contention among many.

He looked down at his plate. The white-bread hoagie was grey at the bottom, soaked with grease from the meat, which was ground chuck mixed with onion, catsup, and Worcestershire sauce. The hoagie had little brown sesame seeds. David took one bite. He did not like sesame seeds. They seemed pointless and he wasn't quite sure where they came from. What was a sesame?

Rose gave him what could have passed for a smile. Then the familiar shadow crossed her face; the smile faded.

"I didn't know you were working today," David said. Which she would either take as a polite nothing, or an accusation that she never told him what was going on. The usual marital mine field.

She shrugged. "Maybe I was, maybe I wasn't."

She was; he knew it, and she knew he did. She was wearing that old black T-shirt and sporting a bruise, so she'd been working somewhere—raiding a lab, freeing go-rillas, saving horses, going wherever the animal rights or-ganizations needed heavy artillery. She met an amazing number of very nasty people, many of them dangerous, and seemed quite satisfied to beat the crap out of anybody who had the bad sense to get in her way. David looked at her, wondering, as he often did, how such a petite, fine-boned woman could be so deadly. He'd seen her kill a man once—a man who had broken into the house and threatened the children. He still remembered what the man's neck bone sounded like when it snapped.

"Where's the poor, orphaned animal?" David asked.

"There isn't always an animal, David."

Mel swallowed a mouthful of roll. "This from the woman who brought home an ostrich."

"I really would like to know what happened to that bird."

David and Mel carefully avoided looking at each other. David flicked a finger at the bruise on her cheek.

"You should put ice on that."

Mel went to the refrigerator door, demanded ice from the side pocket.

"Don't want it," Rose said, chewing hard.

David looked at her, thinking that the chewing must hurt. "Don't pass on the ice just because it was my idea."

Rose frowned at him. Open warfare was a new level, but he wanted new tactics. He was weary of the undertow.

Rose put her hamburger down and went out the back, screen door slamming behind her. A moth scuttled into the kitchen, drawn by the light.

"I get dibs on the couch," Mel said. "Or is that where you're going to sleep?"

THIRTEEN

DAVID WOKE WITH THE SUN IN HIS EYES, AND THE SCREAM of a furious little girl in his ears. Rose's side of the bed had not been slept in. He closed his eyes again, thinking there was something to be said for a bed all to yourself.

He looked at his watch. Seven-thirty. Not much sleep, but it was time to be up and moving. He pulled on his jeans and wandered into the hallway. Mel stood at the edge of the kitchen, hair sticking up, eyes red-rimmed but wide open. Mattie's voice was shrill.

"She ate *all* the Elaki Marshmallow Pops, and yesterday she took the last micro strudel. What am I s'pose to eat?"

Mel scratched his head. "How about I scramble up some eggs?"

David heard a feminine medley of *Oooooo*s, which told him that all his daughters were up.

"Coffee, Mel?"

"Thank God you're up. Where do they get the energy to fight this early in the morning?"

Rose wasn't in the kitchen supervising, obviously. Mattie, Lisa, and Kendra looked sleepy-eyed and grumpy. Lisa sat with a book propped by her cereal bowl, oblivious to Mattie's upset over Elaki Pops. Kendra nibbled at a rice cake, watching weight that did not need to be watched. She curled her lip.

"You shouldn't eat that crap anyway, it's full of sugar."

"Don't say 'crap,'" David said, rote parental involvement.

Mattie squinched her eyes. "I can eat all the sugar I want, I don't have a big moon face."

Kendra's eyes filled instantly. "At least I'm not a bean-pole brat."

David patted Kendra's shoulder, careful not to mess his

49

daughter's hair, something he knew from sore experience would cause more havoc than the fight with her sister. "You have a very pretty face, Kendra."

"I do not. I'm fat. I just don't like that brat throwing it up at me."

David looked at his oldest daughter, who was not fat. He was going to have to talk to Rose about this. He picked Mattie up.

"There's leftover hamburger on a roll. Want some of that?"

She nodded, lower lip big.

"Share it with your Uncle Mel. And Mattie?" He set her on the edge of the counter, lowered his voice to a whisper. "Your sister is very sensitive about her weight. I don't want to hear you call her 'moon face' again."

"She called me beanpole brat."

David set his jaw. "Let me put it this way. Any time I hear you tease her about her weight, you get to scrub every toilet in the house. Argue with me, same punishment. Is *that* understood?"

Her eyes widened, chin down. "Yes, sir." Her tone of voice told him to go to hell.

Mel opened the refrigerator. "Come on, Mattie, come and share this with me."

"Not hungry." She hopped off the countertop, little feet thumping the linoleum, and headed out of the kitchen.

"Eat it while you can," David told Mel, and headed out the back door.

The grass was newly trimmed, the ceramic lawn animals jumbled next to the barn. David looked at them suspiciously, and went to make sure they were turned off. They kept the grass trimmed, but he'd never trusted them.

The barn door was open to catch the air, and light filtered in through the slats of wood on the side. David peeped through the doorway.

Rose was curled up in an open stall, head resting on an old moldy hay bale. She was deeply asleep. Alex the cat was curled on top of the bale, head next to Rose's, tail hanging down the side. A small animal was tucked next to

Rose's feet. David moved closer, wondering what she'd brought home this time.

The piglet's eyes were open and glazed over, rheumy with discharge. David thought it must be dead. He crouched close and put a hand on the animal's side. It was soft, not bristly like it would be as the animal matured. Someone had put it into a teeny harness, which had worked its way into the pig's hide as it grew bigger. The tiny heart beat slow and steady, but the piglet did not react when David stroked its side. Not good.

A bowl of dried chow had been mixed with expensive kiwi and strawberry. David grimaced. From the looks of the bowl, the piglet had not been tempted.

Alex greeted him with a deep-throated purr, and he scratched the cat's head. Rose opened her eyes, sighed deeply, gave him a quick glance. She bent over the pig and rubbed its back.

"Come on, little sweetie. Come on and eat." She took a brown lump from the bowl, put it to the pig's mouth.

The piglet made a tiny squeak and blinked.

"This is not an animal?" David said.

"What?" Rose looked worse this morning, face swollen, bruise purplish-black and spreading.

As he said the words, he wondered why he kept at her over this. "Last night you said you hadn't brought an animal home from work. So I guess this isn't an animal."

"Yesterday I was in Chicago checking on the security of a sea park marineland that trains dolphins with Taser-Pocs—illegal and thriving. There are no pigs there. I found this little guy on the way home, about thirty-five miles out Karlton Lane. He'd been staked outside in the sun all day, food bowl dirty and crusted over. See that little harness? They didn't take it off when he outgrew it. It was made for a kitten, and now it's grown into his hide. His owner had him out there with a 'For Sale' sign, but didn't want to let me take him."

"Did you offer to pay?"

Rose shrugged. "I didn't have any money, and if I did

I wouldn't give it to a creep like that. I got him to let me take the pig for free."

David looked at her. "How?"

"I broke his arm. Didn't really mean to bend it back quite that far." She frowned. "I don't think we have to worry about assault complaints. He was too embarrassed at being roughed up by a shrimpy female to make any complaints. And the pig business could get him in trouble."

"No wonder we don't get invited to block parties."

"Don't worry, David. This little guy isn't going to be here very long. He's going to die. So it'll be an animal, but a dead animal."

"No fair, Rose. I didn't say word one about the dog, did I? Or the cat—"

"*You* brought the cat home."

"Not to mention the ferret, countless numbers of bunnies, the iguana, the goat, the calf—"

"Mattie is crazy about that cow."

"For that matter, so am I, but—"

She raised her chin. "You didn't like the ostrich."

"Is there some law that says I have to be grateful for an ostrich on my front porch?"

"He wasn't on the porch, he stayed in the yard."

"Rose, when cute little piglets grow up they weigh over a thousand pounds, give or take an ounce. We can barely afford to keep the animals we've got. Are we going to send the kids to college, or feed pigs?"

"He's a miniature, David. Hundred pounds, tops."

"I feel so much better."

She laughed when he expected anger, and he was annoyed when he heard Mel calling from the kitchen.

"I guess I better go to work."

"Yeah, David, you go on."

It was there, in the tone of voice. Go to work, leave all the problems behind—cranky children, sick animals. The pig squeaked as David headed out the barn door. He paused, frowning at what was left of his garden. He had planted late, then Meat, the dog, had pulled up half the tiny tender green plants. No home-grown produce this year.

The work was calling him. He wanted to look into this business with Annie Trey, he wanted to talk to Miriam. So easy to turn his back and go—it's what he always did.

But the pig squeaked again, and something in that little piggy whimper stopped him cold. In his mind's eye, he saw Kendra crying at the breakfast table, ignoring a pantry full of food she was afraid to eat; Lisa reading and tuning out the world; Mattie, a small ball of fury.

He walked to the kitchen and called his daughters.

They were still in T-shirts and nightgowns, but something about his tone of voice made them appear instantly. They sat at the table, looking wary.

"We have a sick piglet in the barn," David said.

Mattie leaned her chin on her open palm. "Mama brought it home yesterday. Haas is still in Chicago, he can't come look at it."

David ground his teeth, smiled at his daughter. Haas. Rose's good friend and partner. "It just so happens I talked to three experts on saving animals just last night."

"Who?" Kendra looked skeptical. She didn't believe him.

"Cassidy, Valentine, and Annie."

"Who?"

"No more interruptions. Kendra, warm some milk. Lisa, add sugar to the milk."

"How much?"

"Sweet but not icky."

Kendra put a hand on her hip. "Better ask Mattie, she's the sugar expert."

"Fine," David said. "Mattie puts in the sugar. Lisa, find a cup to pour it in. Get it ready and take it to the barn. Where's Uncle Mel?"

"In the shower," Lisa said.

"Uh, did you warn him about—" A bellow of rage and pain echoed through the hallway. "You guys get the milk ready. I'll go rescue Uncle Mel from the iguana."

FOURTEEN

THE CHILDREN WATCHED, QUIET AND BIG-EYED, AS DAVID curled up beside the bale and took the piglet in his lap. Rose was in the kitchen, summoned to the phone, and David breathed easier out from under her critical eyes. His daughters were still impressed enough to assume he knew what he was doing, but Rose wasn't.

David checked the temperature of the milk on the inside of his wrist, stroked the piglet's rose-petal ear while he waited for the warm, sweet liquid to cool.

Lisa tucked her book under her arm, holding her place with a finger. "We should give it a name. If it has a name, maybe it won't die."

Kendra nodded, biting her lip. "Daddy should name it. He never gets to name the animals."

Mattie sat beside him, put her thumb in her mouth. She had not sucked her thumb since kindergarten, David thought. What did he expect, with Rose throwing dishes at him every time he walked in the front door? Not one of the kids had ever commented. They just sucked their thumbs, decided not to eat, escaped into books.

Kendra sighed. "Earth to Daddy, we need a name. Don't let the milk get cold. I don't want to have to go back in and heat it up again."

David dipped a finger in the cup and held a drop of milk to the pig's snout.

No response. He put more milk on his finger, and coated the thin, pale pink lips. The pig opened its eyes. A small tongue flicked toward his finger, taking one drop of sweet warm milk. The pig licked its lips, looked up at David.

"Hey, little guy. That taste good?"

"He's eating it!" Mattie whispered.

David fed the pig, drop after drop. The pig sat up suddenly, snuffled, teetered toward the bowl on weak, chubby legs, then collapsed face-down in the hay, squeaking.

"Easy little guy." David put the bowl under the pig's chin, and the pig stuck its snout in the bowl and lapped.

"He's getting it on his head," Lisa said.

Mattie reached out and touched the pig's ear. "What's his name, Daddy?"

"Pid."

"Pid? Like Mattie's security blanket?"

Mattie's eyes went soft, and she put a hand on the pig's head. "Pid the pig."

The piglet finished the milk and moved on to the bowl of fruit and chow.

"You got miniature dinosaurs out here too, or is it safe to come in?"

David looked up. Waved a hand at Mel. "You put disinfectant on that scratch?"

"You bet I did. Listen, David, I hate to interrupt this episode of *Animal Farm*, but we got to go to work."

David looked at Kendra. "You kids go in and get dressed. I want you to feed this pig every couple of hours. Milk, like this; then we'll give him more chow tonight. Pid, say hello to your Uncle Mel."

Mel shoved the cat sideways, and sat on the bale of hay. "Pid the pig? And listen, I'm not playing uncle to that pig, so forget it."

"How do you play uncle to a pig?" David said. Pid nosed his arm, and settled back in his lap.

"Like that, I think. You coming or what?"

David frowned, wondering if they should go into the office or straight to Miriam's. "You talk to Miriam's sister yet?"

"Just called her. She says she hasn't heard from Miriam, but she isn't worried."

"She friendly?" David asked.

"Cordial, I guess."

David shrugged. "You know sisters. If one robs a bank, the other hides the loot and gives an alibi. So if you make one of them mad, the other's going to hit you. Did she seem cold?"

"Not so much cold as weird. But you know, we got history there, so it's hard to figure."

David stroked the pig's back, running a fingertip along the leather harness embedded in the hide. "What did you and Miriam really fight about?"

Mel opened his arms. "I told you last night, toilet seats."

"You haven't spoken for two weeks, her sister's acting weird, and she doesn't return your calls. Sounds like more than toilet seats to me."

Mel rolled his eyes. "All I did was ask her not to slam the lid, and she freaked. Started crying; I mean it was silly."

"You say that?"

"What?"

"That it was silly."

"Hell, no. I look stupid?"

"Maybe it was something else. You been getting along lately? She been acting upset?"

Mel bent down, gave the pig a pat. "See, I have a philosophy about women, and up to now, it was working pretty good."

"Up till now?"

"Last few weeks Miriam's been really weird."

"Weird how?"

"It's hard to put my finger on. Say, like we go out to eat and she says she's got to have Chinese, she's craving eggrolls, right? We get there, sit down after a forty-minute wait, then she's like, can't stand the smell, doesn't want Chinese, wants to leave and go for Italian. I figure she's trying to pick a fight. And I'm no doormat, but, I don't know. I don't get mad. She looks tired these days, gets upset over little things. I been trying to go easy, but I got to tell you, I have to watch every word comes out of my mouth."

"She working long hours?"

"Always—you know Miriam—but she don't complain, loves the work. But now she's falling asleep at the movies and stuff, so she's tired or I'm boring as hell, and we know that's not it. Plus she's had some kind of stomach virus, can't seem to shake it. Throws up all the time.''

"Anything else?''

"I don't know. That's not enough? I mean, all of a sudden she's insecure. Asks me do I love her, and how much— like am I going to be any use in a crisis or something. Usually a woman talks like that, you think, oh, marriage hints. But that's not it.''

"You sure?''

Mel shrugged. "I offered, and she turned me down.''

"Sorry.''

Mel waved a hand. "I just asked 'cause I thought it would make her happy.''

David looked at him, wondering if he should be the one to tell his partner that Miriam was pregnant. He wondered how Mel was going to take being a dad.

FIFTEEN

DAVID NOTED THE LEVEL OF DUST IN MIRIAM'S LIVING room and realized that things were very wrong. Mel's instincts had been right; they should have gone straight to her apartment last night. He went to the kitchen sink, dragged a finger across the stainless steel, dipped into the drain and the garbage disposal. Mel stood in the doorway, back against the doorjamb.

"Dry?"

David nodded. He opened the refrigerator.

"She don't cook," Mel said.

"Not much to cook with."

Inside were fruit juices, boxes of soda, fridge crackers.

"The lettuce test?" Mel said.

David nodded and opened the vegetable bin. Sure enough, a head of lettuce, going liquid in the package. Mel looked over David's shoulder, said "shit" under his breath, and left.

David stood up, narrowed his eyes, considered the appliances. Clocks were usually best, especially when they kept the right time. Refrigerators talked too much, and stoves tended to complain. He checked the clock on the wall against his watch—right on the mark. He checked the back for the serial number, then leaned against the counter.

"Police authorization code B7428 addressing appliance Miriam number 8X2BY. Please report last observed activity."

A crackle of static, then the voice of the clock, female, tired, irritable. David wondered who had modeled the voice, and why she had been in such a bad mood.

"Subject owner Miriam Kellog last seen in kitchen, nine-oh-seven P.M., dipping a chocolate bar into a jar of crunchy peanut butter and drinking box of Orchard peach juice."

David grimaced. Pregnant all right. "Date last seen?"

The voice hesitated.

David could close his eyes and imagine a sigh. "You have something else you need to do? Some place to go?"

The clock whirred. "Do not understand the relevance of the question."

He knew better; sarcasm blew the discs on these things. "When was it that you saw Miriam eating the chocolate and peanut butter?"

The clock answered and David checked the date on his watch. Miriam had last been seen by the clock the night Luke Cochran disappeared.

He opened cabinets, browsing. The pantry was obviously stocked by a single person who ate out a lot—olive oil, Thai seasonings, but no common, everyday food packages for the microwave. No boxes of milk, no cereal, but yes on a bottle of champagne.

He opened the jar of peanut butter, almost dropped it when the microchip in the lid activated.

"Sixteen grams of fat for two tablespoons, one hundred and ninety calories."

Was it his imagination, or did the voice seem disapproving? No wonder Kendra was afraid to eat.

There were traces of chocolate in the peanut butter. David wondered where Miriam was, and if she had access to chocolate. He tightened the lid of the peanut butter and headed into the living room.

The room seemed bigger than it was—beige carpet, thick, new looking, a minimum of simple furniture, white verticals over a large window at the end of the room. A computer console sat on the desk, a large slab of glass supported by tubular metal legs. A smudged brown packet sat next to the laptop. David picked it up. Thick. The flap was open and David emptied the contents onto the dusty glass desktop.

Autopsy photos, Annie Trey's infant son. David's stomach dropped. He shoved the photos back into the envelope, pausing over one.

The baby lay on the stainless-steel examining table,

wrapped in a white cotton blanket. The face was unmarked, eyes gummed shut. A pretty baby, with a light fuzz of blond hair.

David put the picture away, sat down on the couch. Annie Trey was dark. He wondered if Luke Cochran had blond hair.

Some days he hated his job.

The quiet hum of appliances never quite at rest got to him suddenly. He headed for the bedroom.

Mel stood beside the bed, looking through the blinds out the window. He held a piece of yellow paper in one hand. There was a stillness about him that David found disturbing.

David looked around the room, feeling like an intruder. He'd worked with Miriam for years; she was the medical examiner of choice. He had not known, during these years, that her bed was low to the floor, king-sized, with a lacy pale blue bedspread, that a ball cap hung on the bedpost.

He pictured her—small-boned, hair fine, long, reddish brown, always coming loose from the French braid or the ribbon that held it back. She had dark eyebrows, a face that was interesting, almost pretty. She was a good forensic technologist, intuitive, methodical, always doing that extra bit of work that separated a good human operator from the computer-generated routine. She and Mel had been circling each other for years—smart remarks, arched eyebrows, sexual innuendo. It was clear to everyone who worked with them that they should either be dating or killing each other.

They had gone out once or twice, early on, until something happened to put an end it—what exactly, Mel never said. From the hints Miriam let drop, David gathered that Mel might have made the mistake of hitting on her sister.

So there had been three years of sniping and open warfare before they were both between relationships and ready to try again.

"Mel?"

Mel looked away from the window. "None of this makes any sense." He sounded calm enough. It would take someone who knew him well, someone like David, to catch the undercurrent burr of roughness. "There's no mail, no newspapers. Somebody's put all that on hold."

"She hasn't been in the kitchen since Cochran disappeared."

Mel nodded. "I took a look at her makeup and stuff, clothes in the closet and dresser. She didn't pack up and go anywhere. Bathroom's a mess—makeup and stuff, pantyhose, wads of tissue, like she got ready in a hurry."

David pointed to the sheet of paper in Mel's hand. "What's that?"

"This?"

"Yeah." David reached for it, and Mel hesitated, then handed it over.

"Looks like a list of my good points. Assets and liabilities, like that."

David read the paper. The heading said MEL THE MAN, and everything was in Miriam's handwriting; David recognized the slant of her tall, spidery scribbles. One side was labeled THE GOOD and the other THE NOT SO GOOD. She had put it a lot kinder than Rose would have.

Mel shook his head, as if he were listening to something high-pitched and uncomfortable. "David, have you ever sat down and listed a woman's good and bad points?"

"No, Mel."

"I mean, either they got tits or they don't, hypothetically speaking. Women, jeez, they're obsessive—how do they have time to even think up all this shit? You think maybe she just had a night where there was nothing good on cable?"

David cleared his throat and read out loud. " 'He makes me laugh.' "

"Don't do that. Don't read it."

" 'He has crinkles around his eyes.' " David looked up. "You know, Mel, I never noticed that, but you do."

"That's like number two on the list of *good* things. Crinkles. I mean, you think this is in order of importance?"

David read ahead. "Not bad, Mel. I never really thought about your butt that way."

"That's good to hear."

"And I had *no* idea—"

"All right, already. Jeez, do we have to enter this in evidence?"

" 'Not punctual and drinks too much. Bachelor for a long time. Set in his ways.' "

"You think I drink too much?"

"Maybe, Mel, but your butt makes up for it."

"Thank *you* for clearing that up."

David looked at a notation at the bottom of the page. "You see this part she underlined?"

"Yeah, but I got no earthly idea what she meant."

" 'He sees me,' " David read softly. " 'He sees me and doesn't go away.' "

Mel turned his back to the room, twitched a slat on the window blind. "David, tell me the truth, do you think Miriam's dead?"

David was reminded of Annie Trey, biting her lower lip, asking after Cochran.

"I think the situation's serious, Mel, and you have reason to be worried. But I'm a long way from giving this up."

He waited for the reaction, but Mel just turned, nodded, and gave him a wan smile. "We'll find her."

David nodded.

Mel stuck his hands in his pockets. "What do we do now?"

In all the years David had partnered with the man, Mel had never asked what to do.

David kept his voice matter of fact. "The point of intersection is Annie Trey. Miriam was working on the Trey infant's autopsy."

"She was trying to prove Annie Trey was innocent."

"She told you that, Mel?"

"Not in so many words. It's the impression I got."

"I'd like to see her lab notes."

"And she disappears same night as Cochran. Probably *with* Cochran."

David nodded. "So we follow the Cochran thing, and we find out who stopped her mail and newspapers."

"You got to know this Cochran is dead, David."

"Doesn't mean Miriam is."

Mel would not meet his eyes. "You got any idea what she meant by that thing she said? That I saw her, and didn't go away?"

David had been married a long time. He knew what Miriam meant. He also knew he couldn't explain it.

SIXTEEN

DAVID WALKED DOWN THE HALLWAY TOWARD THE HOM-
icide bullpen, wondering if Mel had been kidding, or if
everyone had known about him and Teddy. He told himself
not to be self-conscious.

The shift was well underway, almost every desk manned.
Conspicuously unoccupied were String's standing work sta-
tion and Della's desk, computer glowing, chair pushed back
and sideways.

Everyone looked up when David and Mel walked into
the room. There was a long, perceptible pause. David felt
his mouth go dry, and he knew his face was turning red.

A voice came from the hallway, muted but distinct.
Della, her voice up an octave.

"String, you knew about this kind of thing, you should
have *warned* me. I'm a baby when it comes to Elaki romance, I don't—"

"This all new territory, with the human involvement.
Think of this to be an enhancement." String's tones were
an urgent mumble.

"*Enhancement?* You call chemical pheromones—"

David saw Captain Halliday's office was dark. Just as
well.

"This office is getting as bad as your kitchen," Mel said.

David shrugged. "Nobody threw anything when we
walked through the door."

Mel turned sideways, head tilted back. "Has it come to
this, David? You find happiness when you come through a
door and nobody's trying to take your head off with the
crockery?"

"Mel? I know you're upset about Miriam. I know everything else seems like penny-ante bullshit. But—"

"Save the lecture, I've heard it before."

64

David sighed. Was everyone going to be pissy today?

String's voice rose and fell in the hallway.

David went through the bullpen, the haphazard scatter of desks and computers that psychologists claimed would increase productivity more than neat rows. Any increase in productivity was lost in the time it took detectives to negotiate the maze. One guy had gotten so pissed one night, he stood on his desk, beat his chest, and used the other stations as stepping stones to get to the door.

The captain hadn't been around that day either.

David stuck his head in the hallway, saw Della, hair neatly back in a wrapped wedge. For a minute he thought of Detective Yo-Free, Arson, now deceased.

His irritation with Della faded, and he was able to be gentle. "Your hair looks good today."

She frowned, eyes bright with tears. *"What?"*

"I said your hair looks good today. And I like your shirt. I like white cotton shirts. I'm thinking of collecting them."

"David, what is going on with you, you trying to psyche me out?"

"Maybe I just want your shirt."

She rolled her eyes and turned back to String. "This means everything is a fake, it's all—"

"Della?" David said.

"What now?"

"Conference room, please. You can talk to String where everyone in the bullpen can't overhear. And who knows, we might even exchange a few words on the Cochran case."

Della put her hands on her hips, twisted sideways so she could look at him eye to eye. "The conference rooms are full of visiting Elaki dignitaries from DEA, I have been here since five A.M. getting the statement from Cochran's car, and String and me have been *whispering*, so what's your *problem*?"

Mel scratched his head. "This Homicide or junior high?"

"Junior high," David said. "Let's go talk in the principal's office."

"Principal what?" String slid sideways.

"This way," David said, leading them into Halliday's glassed-in cubicle.

"Where's the captain?" Mel said as they passed through the darkened doorway. "Lights up."

The air conditioner compressor kicked on and a radio began to play.

"Air yes, radio no, lights *on*." Mel looked at David. "I thought he got this fixed?"

David settled behind Halliday's desk. Mel and Della exchanged looks.

"Don't get delusional there, David," Mel said.

David leaned back in the chair, waiting for String to find a corner and be still.

The Elaki skittered sideways, shedding scales. "She does not know for the hormone usage enhancement. Do you gentlemens think—"

"Drop it, String." Della's voice was steel-edged.

"What, you want privacy now, after screaming this stuff out in the hallway?"

"Mel—"

"What about the car?" David said.

Della sat on the love seat, swung a leg over the edge. "There were three of them, three Elaki."

String became still. "This traveling of threes is significant."

"Significant how?" David said.

"Is not the natural grouping, unless there is belligerence involved. Three of the grouping is Elaki strong arm technique up none to the good."

Mel leaned back in his chair. "Elaki goon squad? Boggles the mind, don't it?"

String waved a fin. "Is not goon the small furry child cartoon?"

Della shook her head. "No, those fuzzy red things are loons, not goons, y'all pay attention. So around this car we got Elaki goons. Car says Cochran got in first, in the back seat."

Mel pursed his lips. "Forced in, then."

Della nodded. "Car couldn't tell, but sounds like it. Cochran had the car programmed just for him, but he gave it a release, let the Elaki do what they want."

David nodded. Forcibly, then.

"But, David, then it gets weird." Della pulled her leg in, sat forward. "Car says at that point a woman approached. And, I mean, it's hard to put together here, because you know it all gets mixed in with oil pans and navigational stuff, but I think what happened is they put this woman in the trunk, and . . . Mel?"

"I'm okay."

David looked at his partner, saw his face had gone chalk-white. He glanced at Della. "You able to ID this woman?"

Della shook her head. "Probably get something physical out of the trunk, if we turn up a body."

"The car say anything that makes you think there *is* going to be a body?"

"David, they put this girl in the trunk, okay? Not a benevolent act. But get this: According to the car—which was kind of pissy over it—this woman tears a hole in the back of the trunk and crawls into the cab of the car. Proceeds to start whacking the Elaki with a tire iron or something. That's what caused the accident on that exit ramp."

Mel looked at David, eyes deep-set and circled, a tired grin on one side of his mouth. " 'Atta girl."

SEVENTEEN

THE POLICE GARAGE WAS WELL LIGHTED, CAVERNOUSLY large, hot. Huge fans blew air through the concrete shell, turning it into a wind tunnel. Conversation took volume and perseverance. Voices echoed, and tools clanged on the oil-stained concrete.

Luke Cochran's black Visck was up on blocks, doors open, trunk lid up, lights on. One of the tires had been removed. The forensic mechanic stood to one side, talking to a male apprentice. She wore a Greek fisherman's cap turned backward, her shoulder's were slumped, hands hanging loose. She was overweight, her hair tied back with a thick white rubber band.

"Two kinds of cookies," the apprentice was saying. He was young, probably just out of school. His hair was neatly razor cut, his shoulders wide, hips slim. "How about one macadamia nut and one oatmeal raisin?"

David looked at the set of the mechanic's shoulders, the way her hands hung by her sides. She was unhappy about something. She would want chocolate chip.

"You go ahead, I'm not hungry." She caught sight of them over the boy's shoulder. "Kevin, this is Detective Silver, Burnett, and String. You know Della."

"String?" the boy said.

"That would be the Elaki," Mel said. Kevin blushed and ducked his head.

String slid toward the car. "Have there been much scatter of scales, Vanessa?"

The woman tilted her hat farther back on her head. " 'Bout a million and one, up front. Sam's already been here, getting samples to double-check his results. I think maybe he found something weird."

"Weird how?" David said.

68

She shrugged. "Dunno."

"You had much of a chance to look at the car?"

"Yeah. And Della, you were right. Sam thought the same thing and I had no trouble establishing casebook confirmation, if we need it for court. Somebody went through the trunk here, up into the cab."

Mel and Della moved around the car, peering into the trunk.

"You have found something to interest the tires?" String asked.

Vanessa grinned. "Let's say the tires interest me. It's just a routine check, soil samples, broken glass, gravel. You know the drill. We're not likely to find a damn thing, but you never know. You guys find this Cochran yet? Got any leads, come up with a body?"

Mel cleared his throat.

Vanessa put her hands in her pockets. " 'Cause if there's any chance the kid's alive, I can give you a holographic reconstruction. If you're stuck for leads and you got the budget, this one's a good candidate. Nav program still intact, I can probably give you the whole blow by blow."

David looked at Mel, then Vanessa. "Let me check with the captain—"

"David." Mel's voice was unusually quiet. "If we learned nothing else in all our years of punting red tape, it's don't ask a question when you don't want an answer. My guess is that if we tell Vanessa here that Miriam Kellog may be involved—"

Vanessa's hands went deeper into her pockets. "Miriam? I did a seminar with her at the university."

Mel nodded. "So if we were to ask you to go all out on this, we could kind of pass the buck around on the approval, and let the shit fall."

"Chips fall," String said. "This be the expression."

"String, it's just short for 'shit chips,' so don't be correcting me."

Della folded her arms. "Vanessa, what was it Sam Caper was double-checking?"

"Something in the trunk. Matching blood samples on the seat in the back."

EIGHTEEN

THE ELEVATOR WAS HOT, AND DAVID, CRAMMED NEXT TO String, Della, and Mel, wished he'd opted for the stairs. He took a breath, stuck a finger in his shirt collar. He looked at Della and String, wondered what the big commotion in the hallway had been about. Something to do with Della's love life, and he knew she was seeing an Elaki. What had String said about enhancements? He closed his eyes, speculating on sexual incompatibility.

"David?" Mel's voice.

"Yeah?"

"Our floor, which you would know by now if you'd open your eyes."

David walked off the elevator, saw a thin, blond woman standing by his desk. For an instant he thought it was Teddy. It only took a second's focus for him to realize that the similarity was nothing more than wishful thinking working overtime.

David glanced back at Mel. "Not getting off?"

"I want to talk to that Caper guy."

"He'll call when he gets results," David said.

"I know. I'm going up there anyway."

The elevator door asked if everyone was ready or not, and closed.

David looked at String. "Check up on Miriam's last movements. When she was last seen, you know the drill. See if you can get anything out of her sister. She's a beat cop. Works out of the Carlton First."

"She has not been to report the Miriam pouch-sib to be missing?" String said.

"Mel says not."

"Isss interesting this."

70

Della frowned. "You want me to stay with background on this Cochran kid?"

"Hit hard on the finances. That's an expensive car he was kidnapped in."

"It's his too; I checked."

David nodded. "Meanwhile, his girlfriend, Annie Trey, holds her breath when she goes through the checkout line at the grocery store, unless I've misjudged that one."

"Want me to look into her?"

"She's the connection between Luke Cochran and Miriam."

"Both of whom are now missing. Wonder who the father is on that baby that died."

David scratched his chin. "Newspapers never were able to dig that up."

"I look like a newspaper hack to you? Look, we'll talk later. You got a visitor, don't keep her waiting."

David headed for the blonde.

She was thin, shoulders narrow, hair hanging down her back. She got older the closer David got. There was a stoop to her shoulders, a shyness in the way her arms hung tight to her sides that made her seem younger at a distance. But lines of hard living and late-night worries showed across the tan, freckled forehead, and around the mouth and neck. She had a double chin where the skin in her neck had sagged, flaccid and tired. Her hair was cut in short bangs, and everything about her—from the cheap plastic sandals to the crooked, uncared-for teeth, bespoke years of poverty and living on the edge. The shape of the jaw, the wide-set eyes, gave her an inbred look that kept her from being pretty.

David smiled, trying for warmth, and failing. He went around the back of his desk, but stayed on his feet.

"I'm Detective Silver, ma'am. Can I help you?"

She nodded when she heard his name, clutched the strap of her purse. "They said downstairs you was the one to talk to. I'm Tina Cochran?"

She had the kind of accent that gave Southerners a bad name.

"Cochran? Luke's mother?"

"I'm his mama, yes. Thank you for *not* saying 'next of kin.'"

David shook her hand. Her skin was cool, and her bones felt tiny and fragile. The look in her eyes was eager for all that it was anxious, and David felt a prick of alertness. She was worried and afraid and ready to tell him anything in the hopes he might find her son.

Conference room C, he decided, just the two of them.

"Can I get you some coffee?" he asked.

NINETEEN

TINA COCHRAN WAS NOT MUCH FOR COFFEE, BUT SHE TOOK the cold red box of Coke with a smile of gratitude that made David decide she'd had very few pleasures in life. The look in her eyes made him go back out for a vending raid, and he came back with candy bars and potato chips and a feeling of foolishness, till he saw the red flush of pleasure on her cheeks.

Something about this woman made him want to be nice.

She sat on the edge of her chair, carefully opening a chocolate caramel cinnamon wafer.

"The wrapping on these is so pretty," she said, talking fast and breathless. "I like this brown on black, and the gold stripe. Makes you wonder who thought it up."

She'd be a cheap date, came the nasty voice in David's mind.

"A detective Thurmon called me last night, Detective Silver. He says y'all found my boy's car."

David nodded. Tina Cochran took a bite of wafer, chewed the caramel slowly. Swallowed.

"But you didn't find him?"

David leaned forward. "Detective Thurmon didn't—"

"Look, he don't like me, he don't tell me a thing." She put the candy bar down, wiped her hands on her shorts. Small round chocolate fingerprints dotted the material across her stringy thighs.

"We found his car near Elaki-Town. It had gone over a guardrail on the exit ramp."

She pressed the back of her hand across her mouth, but did not utter a sound.

"The car wasn't smashed too badly; it didn't look—" David hesitated.

"Fatal?" Tina Cochran said.

David rubbed a hand across the back of his neck. "What I'm trying to say is, I don't think your son would have been killed by the impact."

Her eyes narrowed. David noticed flecks of yellow in the brown.

"Go on," she said. "There's more."

"We did find blood in the car. Our CSU guys are testing right now to see if it's his. And we found . . . a tennis shoe that has been identified as belonging to your son."

"By who?"

"Pardon?"

"Who said that the shoe there was his?"

"His girlfriend. Annie Trey."

"You called her and not me?" I'm his *mama*, her voice said.

"We should have called you," David said. "That was a mistake."

"I guess she was the one called the trouble in. So she's the one you knew to call."

She was consoling him, David realized. She was all hard angles, high cheekbones and knobby knees, but the impression she gave was soft.

"You don't know then, Detective Silver, if he's dead or alive?"

"Not yet. But I will."

She looked at the floor. Kneaded the cuffs of her shorts. "Tell you the truth, I don't know what's worse. Not knowing, or finding him dead."

He wanted to pat her shoulder, but didn't know her well enough.

She rose up off the edge of her chair. "Well, thank you much for your help."

"Don't go," David said. "I'd like to ask a few questions, if you think you have the time."

Wariness hit her like a wave, and she turned sideways in the chair, smile fading. "What you want to know?"

If he'd learned nothing else, David knew when to bide his time. "Where he was born, where he grew up . . . how the two of you got along."

The last one stirred her, and she flipped her hair back over her shoulder and balled her hands into fists.

"Luke was the sweetest, caringest son a mama could ever have. We had those teenage-year problems, but all families do, rich or poor, Detective. He sassed me some, and he stayed out late, and he let his schoolwork slide. But he made it to college. Luke is what you call a survivor. Always lands on his feet. He works hard, and he tries to give me money all the time. Makes him mad 'cause I won't take it, but he's got tuition to pay, discs, and books."

"So he's generous," David said, pretending to make a note. And he thought, again, of the car.

"Always trying to give me something."

David scratched his cheek. "Is he working his way through school?"

She nodded, shoulders back. "And you must know how hard that is. Not every boy would work so hard. Last time I saw him, he was so tired he couldn't eat. Came for dinner, then fell asleep watching the TV. And that was eight o'clock at night. We're talking about a boy who likes to stay up late and have his fun—falling asleep by eight at night."

"What does your son do?" David asked.

She was still wrapped up with the martyred child, and at first did not comprehend the question. "What do you mean, what does he do? For fun, you mean, or—"

"For a living. How is he working his way through school? Are you helping him?"

"No. I wish I could, but I barely pay my own bills. It gets down to groceries some weeks." Her voice was soft and hard to hear.

"Does Luke have a job?"

Her chin lifted, but she would not meet his eyes, and her skin went dark pink across her cheeks.

"Ma'am?"

"He works, yes."

"Where?"

"At school. The university. Some kind of work-study program."

"What does he do?"

"I don't know exactly. Lab work, I think, for one of the teachers. I don't know the ins and outs; I didn't get my high-school diploma."

David studied her, letting the silence fill the room. With or without the high-school diploma, she was an intelligent woman, and shrewd. It was an old trick she was using, one that probably worked well. Her accent was thick, her hands callused, that hungry look in her eyes eloquent. People would let her get away with playing dumb.

"Mrs. Cochran, I'm a little . . ." David hesitated, scratched his head. "I guess I'm puzzled, so maybe you can help me out." *Two playing dumb*, went the voice in his head. "I have to say I'm impressed that he's got the stuff to work his way through school, and I admire that. I'm sure you've raised a fine boy."

She chewed a lip, the trace of a nervous smile coming and going.

"But how can he afford tuition and books, and a car as expensive as the one he had? How can he afford to offer you money?"

In a split second, she was up out of the chair, leaning over him. "I didn't say I took his money. He's got a job at the school. And sometimes I do give him something." She went red again, to the roots of her hair. "What are you trying to say, anyhow?"

He shook his head at her slowly, and she took a step backward and bit her lip. Overreacting, David thought. He was on the right track.

"I'm not trying to *say* anything, Mrs. Cochran. It's an expensive car, that's all."

"He didn't steal it."

"Of course not. Sit down, please."

"Why should I sit down? Why should I let you make him out to be some kind of bad guy? My *boy* disappeared, he's been gone for days, not a call, not a note, not a message." David saw the tears film her eyes, and he felt tired suddenly, muscles tight and achy."

"Please, Mrs.—"

She sat down suddenly. "When he was two years old I used to take him to the park every day before lunch. And if he'd fall off the slide or get hurt on the swing, he'd come running across that playground and grab my knees." She wiped her nose with the back of her hand. "It was me he needed, his mama, and back then I could make it all better. But kids grow up, and they quit looking at you like you're the one person who has all the answers. And I don't. I don't have all the answers. How come you don't ask me about any of the good stuff?"

"I'm asking you right now."

"What?"

"About the good stuff. Tell me."

He saw it in her face, the urge to sit and indulge in an orgy of stories about her son. But she shook it off, the temptation, and David felt disappointment and relief.

"I got nothing else to say."

That in itself was interesting. "I see."

"I mean that. Can I go, please?"

David nodded. "If you decide you have more time to talk, here's my card. Just ask, it'll tell you the number."

She took the card, nodded stiffly.

David looked at the pile of candy. "Nobody here eats much chocolate," he lied. "You might as well take those along."

He had meant to be kind, but it was the wrong thing to say.

Tina Cochran lifted her chin. "Thanks, but I couldn't. And I can *read* your card, it doesn't have to talk."

David watched her go, wondering if Luke Cochran was dead or alive, and in what particular flavor he was dirty.

TWENTY

DAVID SAT ALONE IN THE CONFERENCE ROOM, THINKING. He did not feel well. He was hot all over, had an odd tightness in his chest. Tired, he decided, and got up to leave, colliding with Della in the hallway.

"David? I been looking for you. Mel just got back from the lab."

Something in her voice stopped him cold. "Miriam?"

"Definite match. Blood from her and from Cochran."

"Okay. Get Mel down here. Grab String." He felt a throb of pain like a noose tightening around his temples, and he grabbed the door handle.

Della was halfway down the hallway. "We're not on the schedule for C, Silver, let's move our stuff upstairs."

"Just get them," David said. He took a breath. Coffee, he thought. He and Mel could use a pot.

"It's what we expected, Mel." David handed him a cup of coffee. His partner was stiff-shouldered, movements slow and jerky, mind everywhere but there.

Mel looked at the cup of coffee. "No thanks." He took a sip.

"Sugar?" David asked.

"Black is fine." Mel took another swallow, folded his hands on the table. Stared at his sleeves.

The door opened and String slid through, the door catching his bottom fringe and scattering scales.

"Have talk to this Capering Sam in the lab of bits of bone." David winced, but Mel did not register. "And this blood of the Miriam is in quantities very small."

Della put her fingertips together, spotted the chocolate, gave it a second look, then turned to Mel. "The car hit the guardrail, so she's banged up just a little. Chances are good she's still alive.''

Mel's voice was flat. ''If she's still alive, where the hell is she? Lookit. She's supposed to meet this Cochran kid and Annie Trey. Why at night like that, after dark?''

Della shrugged. ''Annie works, Luke is in school. Miriam herself is on leave and working out of her apartment and the university lab.''

''But why meet with them? She's going out of channels, talking directly to them like that. Something funny there; something's not right.''

''Is the funny odd, yes please.'' String was still this morning, not jittering around. Mel and the Elaki were both weirdly calm, while David could hardly bear sitting still. His back ached, and he shifted his weight. He shivered.

''David?'' Della said.

He looked up dully.

''It *is* funny about that. Her talking out of channels, like Mel said.''

David moved sideways in his chair. ''She doesn't seem to think Annie did it. I looked through some of the stuff at her desk, gave her computer discs to Sam. She seemed to be looking for a virus or a bacterium, as opposed to a toxin of some kind. So she must have already ruled poison out.''

String's eye prongs twitched. ''What is thing that the Miriam could find to justify the nighttime meet? To talk to the Annie direct?''

''What hospital Annie say she took her baby to?'' Mel asked.

''Meridian branch of University,'' Della said.

David looked at String. ''Your chemaki mate still working in the ER?''

''Yes, Aslanti work all the hours, but this is at Bellmini Hospital.''

''Yeah, but I bet she hears the scuttlebutt. She familiar with the Trey case?''

''Much of the gossip, no fact.''

''Which is?''

String slid back and forth across the floor. ''That baby

die very sick, very fast, of no known disease. That poison
not be detected, but odd bodily damage found. Still trying
to detect source. Some weird hush hush, no one can
be understood. People discouraged from getting the involvement, when opposite would normally be. But medical
opinion is that the autopsy be for the benefit of mother, to
prove innocence. Doctors do not think she be culpriting
here. Dissatisfaction with media big and fat.''

"So nobody on the medical side thinks Annie Trey was
involved?" Della asked.

"This is just said," String replied.

David rubbed his eyes. "Give Aslanti a call, tell her we-
're coming over. Sweet-talk her, String. Maybe she can
save us some time, if she's willing. Della, how goes the
background on the Cochran boy?"

"Still on it. What I got so far is school schedule, finances, like that."

"And?"

She picked up a chocolate bar, unwrapped it slowly.
"Grew up hard, he and his mother. He was into some
small-time scrapes. Nothing real nasty, just kind of an operator. You know, the kid who steals your hubcaps and sells
them back to you. He'd take the credit tally out of your
wallet, but mail back the pictures of your kids."

"Old habits die hard," Mel said.

David nodded. "What about finances?"

"Preliminary shows he's the typical starving student."

Mel looked up. "How'd he afford the car?"

"That's what I want to know. Della, look into that job
he had at the university, see what they pay."

"They pay him enough for a car like that; I'm apply-
ing."

"String," David said. "That business last night in Elaki-
Town. What was going on there? You got any idea?"

"Hard to be of the sureness. Much tension, odd behavior."

"Let's say we don't believe in coincidence," Mel said.
"We got Cochran's car on the exit ramp leading to Elaki-
Town. Miriam gone. Elaki weird shit all around."

"Eloquent," Della said.

David swallowed. His throat was sore. "Any idea what the connection could be?"

"None in the hereafter," String said. "Must go to see, and carefully."

"Can we use uniforms on the legwork?" Mel asked.

String cocked an eye prong. "No. Must be calling Walker for help."

"Walker?" David looked at Mel.

Mel rolled his eyes. "*Walker?* No. Please. Nada."

"There's got to be another way," Della said.

"She has connections out of the kazoo."

"Wazoo," Mel said.

String twitched an eye prong. "Whatever."

TWENTY-ONE

DAVID BRACED HIMSELF JUST BEFORE STRING DROVE THE
van up onto the curb.

"Will you *please* learn to parallel park?" Mel said.

"This I have done."

"No. Parallel parking is beside the curb, not up on it."
David climbed out of the van. "Where's Walker?"

"Did not wish to arrive together. Will meet at taco shop.
Must do this her way, the old sledgehammer."

David looked at Mel, who shrugged.

"Isss human expression. To mean rough hard difficult
female unattractive."

Mel scratched his chin. "Let's see. One word for—"

"Battleax," David said.

"Kind of like working a crossword puzzle. Hey, David?
You feeling okay?"

David wiped a hand across his forehead. He was sweating—it was hot out, but he felt cold. "Yeah, fine." He
looked up and down the street, hoping the taco shop was
close and he could sit. "String, did she say which taco
shop?"

"No, just the taco shop."

"I count three from where I stand. You sure she didn't
specify?"

"No."

Mel groaned. "We'd have more luck going to Chinatown
looking for a place that serves rice."

String waved a fin. "One by one to be the methodical."

"Can't we just give her a call?"

Elaki-Town was relatively safe in daylight hours, in the
area between Cass Avenue and Nix Street. But the three of

82

them stayed together, walking nonchalantly, keeping a watch on their backs.

The walls were plastered with ads, all of them featuring Elaki selling human products—Elaki without hair selling shampoo, Elaki driving cars, Elaki wearing the latest sweatshirts from Gap Three.

David heard an overwhelming grinding noise and the throb of a large diesel engine as an Elaki tourist boat rolled into the street, stopping traffic.

"What the hell is that?" Mel said.

The boat was red and black, lacquered prow shaped like a dragon. Rows and rows of Elaki crowded the sides, taking video cams. All of them wore red ball caps, identifying them as part of TOURS, RANGER-ROVER. The caps sat behind their eye prongs, and looked uncomfortable. Elaki loved ball caps.

String slid sideways, shedding scales. "Elakitours— many crave the experience yachting. But water has the vice connotations, and Elaki do not do well with the wave roll. So a street-bottomed boat cruise of Elaki-Town, with a small exposure to pretend danger, is much to be desired."

"Looks like a Chinese junk," David said.

The boat passed and the three of them moved on. The streets were maintained fairly well, David decided, in this part of Elaki-Town. Not bad, considering the area—no doubt the Elaki influence. Walkways were narrow, alleys were lined in gravel for no reason David could fathom, and stores were more like stalls—tall, narrow, and crowded. They passed a noodle shop that smelled like cinnamon. An Elaki played an accordion in the middle of the sidewalk, eye prongs bent, scales missing, hide ragged. Someone had put a taco in his bowl. It was wrapped in paper with a logo that said TACO SHOPPE.

David pointed. "A clue."

TWENTY-TWO

THEY FOUND WALKER STANDING OUTSIDE THE TACO Shoppe, muttering something about fairy lights and doughnuts. She did not sound happy.

Nothing new, David thought.

Mel waved a limp hand. "Yo, Mama, how's it hanging?"

Walked hissed. "How is what hanging, Detective Burnett?"

"Uh—"

"As if I do not have the knowledge."

David sighed. This was not getting off to a good start.

Mel squinted at her. "What is it you think you do not have the knowledge of?"

"Is crude reference to drooping prongs."

Mel grinned. "More like drooping d—"

"Mel," David said.

"Yeah, yeah."

"Let's go inside."

David had forgotten that in an Elaki restaurant there would be no chairs. He leaned against the table while everyone went up to get tacos. The food smells made him nauseous, particularly the sweet and tart odor of lime and cinnamon that permeated any area frequented by Elaki. David swallowed hard and wondered if he could stand to watch them eat.

He glanced around the restaurant. The establishments in Elaki-Town were unusual in that they employed Elaki for the scut work, instead of humans. This place was not up to the usual standards of Elaki cleanliness. The walls had been slapped over with sandy-brown stucco. For some reason, the Formica tables were Pepto Bismol-pink—a popular color with the down-at-heel Elaki—a shade that seemed to give them the same muted comfort humans found in beige. The tables were high. The tabletop lined up with David's shoulder blades, giving him a child's eye view. He had to remind himself that he was not in a foreign country.

Mel settled between Walker and String. He opened his taco, took a bite, made a face. Glanced over at David.

"I know these guys put cinnamon in everything right down to their coffee and beer, but this is unbelievable. Take a bite."

David shuddered. "Can we get on with this?"

Walker twitched an eye prong. "The human is sick."

David tapped a finger on the tabletop. "The human has a name. You can call me David, or Detective Silver, or sir. Don't call me the human."

String skittered sideways. "Detective David is not up to the par, so will be somewhat the testicle."

"*Testy*," Mel said. "I think the Elaki attempts comic relief."

String took a bite of taco. David noticed that the Elaki could eat them now without shattering the shell. It was a good indication of how long an Elaki had been on Earth. He hadn't met one yet who did not love tacos. If they could eat without making a mess, they'd been around awhile.

David looked at Walker. "You up to date at all with the Cochran situation?"

"Ssssure, Detective David Silver, sir. I have no life's work but to study you the caseload."

Mel wiped his mouth with a napkin. "You know, Walker, you could be the poster child that spearheads the drive to send every Elaki home. Put you in a couple vids, and donations will start pouring in."

Walker slid sideways, shedding scales, and David hid a smile. She would take Mel's mind off his worries, if nothing else. He wondered why he was so tired, and why it felt so good to be still. Wondered if he was coming down with something awful.

Old age?

Mel took a drink of beer. "Okay. Cochran kid is in his dorm room, talking on the phone to his—"

"I have knowledge for this, I live in the world." Walker picked taco shell out of a breathing slit. "This girlfriend is the Annie Trey who has poisoned the little newborn pouchling." Walker's eye prong twitched. "So admirable the Mother-One."

David felt a rush of heat, wondered if his face was as red as it felt. There was a peculiar tightness in his chest that made him take two or three deep breaths. He swiped a napkin off String's tray, wiped his face.

He made a conscious effort to keep his voice mild. "Annie Trey's been crucified by the media rock, but we're a long way from being sure she's responsible for the death of that baby. There are a lot of things that need looking into."

"Such as be?"

"Such as Cochran," David said. "And Miriam Kellog. She was doing the Trey baby autopsy, and her notes make me think she'd decided Annie Trey got a bad deal. She was going to meet Annie and Luke Cochran the night she disappeared."

"She is disappear? The Kellog Miriam?"

David avoided Mel's look.

"Out of the trunk of Cochran's car," Mel said. "Got bloodstains that match hers and Cochran's. The scenario is Cochran looks out the window in his dorm, sees a couple—"

"Three," String said.

"Yeah, three—"

"Three has the significance." Walker cocked an eye prong in String's direction.

Mel shrugged. "So I been told. Anyways, all of them wind up going for a ride, Miriam in the trunk. We think what happened is Miriam crawls from the trunk into the cab of the car, starts whacking on Elaki with a crowbar, and the car goes over the guardrail and off the ramp. This is the Elaki-Town ramp, which is why we're all here."

String tore a napkin into small pieces, which he balled up and rolled across the table. "Blood in car. Scales, of the many. Shoe cap of Cochran identified by the Trey."

"Tennis shoe," Mel said.

"Do not correct the proper. Shoe cap is best," Walker said.

Mel looked at David. "They never heard the expression *when in Rome*?"

"So the car full of dubious human and pirate Elaki come here for the reason what?" Walker folded her napkin into a precise square.

"That's the question," Mel said.

David's back was aching. He shifted his weight, trying to find relief. "Another thing, Walker. It was very odd here the other night. Tense. String said it was scary enough to rush the physical investigation and bug out."

"Bugs were out?" Walker said.

"Don't play the dumbkin," String said sharply.

David eyed the two Elaki. He had been suspecting for some time now that the constant Elaki misunderstandings were a subtle form of Elaki fun.

String swayed back and forth, and David found the constant motion almost hypnotic. "Elaki out late—no lights, all hush dark. But wait and watch on the doorstep, thick hubrits—"

David looked at Mel. *Hubrits?*

"And quiet the watchful," String said.

"No approachments?" Walker asked.

"No," String said. "And coming here, to find this meeting. Much observation of the human. Hostile."

Walker swayed back and forth, and David noticed she was keeping time with String. Two Elaki in agreement, he thought.

"Hostile the norm," Walker said.

"Norm overflowing," String added.

Mel wadded his trash and stuffed it in a box. "Yeah, I noticed that too. Not the staring so much, but a feeling. Very unfriendly. Nervous, too. You pick that up, David?"

"Yeah," David said. He hadn't, really. He wasn't noticing much of anything all of a sudden. The flush of heat started up again, making him sweat. He shifted his weight again and wished he could sit down.

''I have some contacts for the information. You will question them for knowledge. Is gravel stand, we talk to Brian.''

''Brian? An Elaki named Brian?'' Mel asked.

Walker looked at him oddly. ''So why not?''

TWENTY-THREE

WALKER SWORE THE GRAVEL STAND WAS IN WALKING DIS-
tance, and she rolled ahead of them down the sidewalk
without a backward glance.

Mel moved in close to David. "Something funny here,
David. I mean, you noticed there are no other humans,
none, but us?"

David nodded. He had been noticing just that. The layout
of Elaki-Town had an odd feel—narrow streets, tall thin
stalls, all very cheap. The low-end Elaki market, catering
to fringe elements, criminal or weird or both. A shiny bus,
triple-decker, went slowly past, Elaki standing fin to fin,
holding straps and staring out the window. More upscale
Elaki, fascinated by how the other half adapted to human-
ity—Elaki watching Elaki, with the typical narcissism of
their race.

David saw String exchange looks with Walker, then
swoop behind them, so that Walker went ahead and String
brought up the rear, with Mel and David between them. He
looked to the right, saw storefronts—antique stores, lots of
those, taco stands, coffee stalls, harness outfitters, rip-off
contraptions that would allegedly anchor the aliens in a
strong wind. There were vids, and little vests on display.
The crowds seemed thinner than usual, business slow, a lot
of places closed. And a trio of Elaki across the street, keeping pace.

David frowned. Three meant trouble.

"String's worried," Mel muttered. "Four police officers
in the light of day, and believe me, he's worried. David,
are you listening to me here? You paying attention?"

Walker turned suddenly, moving into a dark storefront,
and David followed Mel, glad to be in off the streets.

The gravel stand reminded David of the delicatessens of

his childhood, minus the cacophony of spicy smells. Motes of dust jittered in the bars of sunlight that came in through a small rectangle at the top of the ceiling, and lay like fine ash on the walls, the floor, the countertop. Inside a glass display case were trays of gravel, some colored, most grey-blue or white, of different sizes and grades, from medium chunks that would bite bare feet, to tiny marbleized sludge-like caviar, and about as expensive. A scale hung from a wall—the old-fashioned balance kind that had been used to weigh fruit and vegetables when David was a boy.

There were prices on the gravel, stuck in the center with a pronged stick, like you'd find in an old-fashioned butcher shop. Voices rose and fell in the back room. Even from the front of the shop the conversation sounded intense—two or three Elaki, voices sharp. David could not make out any words.

The voices stopped, and an Elaki came out of the back room, closed a partitioning door. He was tall, even for an Elaki, and significantly wider—double load. His inner belly was an unhealthy grey, his black outer hide faded, rough and patchy with missing scales.

"This is the snitch of mine," Walker said. "He name Brian, but is called for informal, the Smalls."

Walker slid from side to side, looked at them, made a sharp whistle. "I have given you the snitch introduction. Are there not questions?"

David heard Mel mutter something about Walker and her usual charm. The feeling in his chest was getting worse. He wondered what a panic attack felt like, and if he was having one.

Mel turned sideways. "According to protocol, Walker, he's your snitch, so you're supposed to question him. We're just showing you a little professional courtesy here, but hey, feel free to stand aside and keep your mouth shut."

Brian-Smalls twitched a prong, belly rippling just slightly, but enough to let David know the Elaki was amused.

"Rules of courtesy nonsensical do not interest me. Human bow and scrape of a time-wasting dullness."

"You know, Walker, some snitches won't talk if you're offensive."

"You must have no conversations then, Burnett."

"*Enough*," David said. He rubbed the back of his neck, and the Elaki named Brian-Smalls skittered sideways, an eye prong cocked his way. "We're looking for a human named Luke Cochran."

"Would this relate to the automobile black and sleek, crashed up on the ramping exit?"

David nodded.

"He mean yes," Walker said.

"Yes," David said.

"I know this auto. Belonging to human who does the strange jobs."

"Odd jobs?" Mel said.

"He would be working the antique circuit, mainly with the Sifter."

"The sifter?" David said.

"Sifter. Is Elaki antique dealer. Sells some to Elaki passing through from shop, but main deals in bulk to home planet."

"He sells antiques from Earth to the home planet?" David said.

"Isss big this," String said, waving a fin. "Much is the valuable."

"What, like furniture and folk art?" Mel asked.

Brian-Smalls rolled forward on his fringe. "The used tennis shoe very big. Odd items, for to you, but would be like the folk art for Elaki. Human cooking utensils. Teddy bear, wax fruit, the Pez."

"What is this Pez?" String asked.

David shook his head. "No idea."

Brian-Smalls waved a fin. "I do not know, me this. Just know that Sifter has many times asked for me to be on the lookout."

"What do you know about this Cochran?"

Brian-Smalls moved out from behind the counter, looked out the windows, seemed satisfied.

"This boy in much of the trouble. Has offended deeply.

Has been offered the Sanctuary."

Neither String or Walker said anything, but both went rigid. String moved in closely, and David took a step back.

"You know what it is that you say?"

Brian-Smalls hissed. "I make this up, me this?"

David and Mel exchanged looks.

"The Sanctuary is great offense," String said. "The sharps sales of antiques or business screw around will not be the least justification."

"I do not know of all the details. The antique is not for the problem, and the Cochran was champion of the boss, Sifter, who pulls the heavy weight, him do. This is a blood sanction."

"He kills an Elaki, then?" Walker said.

Brian-Smalls cocked an eye prong her way. "A betrayal. This is all I know. Three were sent to bring him on this night of the crash. But there is disagreement; we do business here, we don't wish to bring this law human trouble on us, or Izicho in flock."

Walker looked at String, but said nothing, to David's immense relief. String was Izicho, Elaki secret police, with no official authority, but a great deal of quiet power among his own. He was not supposed to be active. Walker did not trust him. David did. He also knew String was active.

"What did Cochran do?" David asked.

"This me do not know. Just the blood betrayal. And that night there is much of the consternation, and we close early and some go home, and many others stay. Plenty enough for a quorum."

"A quorum for what?" Mel asked.

"For dealing the penalty."

"There was a woman with him that night," David said.

"The woman does not exist," Smalls said.

Mel choked and moved forward, but David laid a hand on his arm. "You better explain that. Did something happen to her?"

"Nothing happens to no one."

"What about the woman?" Mel asked.

"Nothing happens to no one."

The Elaki slid back behind the display case and Mel started toward him. String scooted forward and headed him off.

"We go."

Mel looked at him.

"We go," String told him. "Please trust."

TWENTY-FOUR

DAVID WENT ALONE TO THE ANTIQUE STORE. WALKER hung back, according to plan, watching the three Elaki who watched him. String and Mel had headed out, over Mel's loud objections, to go through Miriam's professional notes on the Trey autopsy and take them to Aslanti. David wanted an objective opinion, untainted by any police or social work connections. And he wanted Mel out of the way, something String had picked up on right away.

It would be uncomfortable if he had to take Mel off the job.

The Elaki antique shop was very like the human version, dark inside, aisles narrow, too many things crammed into too small a space. Elaki liked to live this way as a matter of course, so it was no surprise that they had taken to selling antiques.

The shop did not look prosperous. From the little David knew about the antique business, this meant Sifter was likely wealthy, and accomplished.

David expected furniture but got teddy bears—rows and rows of them. Winnie The Pooh, Sears tags prominently displayed. Brown bears, with mohair fur, one like a clown with curly white goat hair. They were well-loved, these bears, fur matted and worn. One bear wore a wedding dress. David paused and gave it a second look.

"Golden tan mohair, circa 1983. Made by Gloria Franks. Only one hundred fifty of them be ever made—created on a farm in West of the Virginia. Originally sold for two hundred dollars. If you can imagine."

The Elaki was sleek and well built, even handsome. His eyes were full of fun, and he gave David look for look, unlike most Elaki, who bent an eye prong and moved away. He waved a fin, actually touching David's arm. David had

94

never had an Elaki touch him that way, companionably, like a pal.

My first Elaki salesman, David thought.

"If you like this Gloria tan, I can get you the price better. My name be Chuck, by the by. And you, good sirs?"

"Silver, David Silver. I'm looking for the owner. I'm looking for Sifter."

The Elaki rolled back, then forward. "But you have found me, David Sssilver. I am the Sifter. They calls me Sifter Chuck."

He was not at all what David expected. He had imagined an old Elaki, barely standing, dark and crabbed, grumpy and clipped. Never this youngster, bursting with so much energy he could not stay still. There was something so very likable about him, something that made you want to ask him out for a drink, tell him a joke, hear him laugh. Elaki, of course, did not laugh out loud. But if one ever did, David thought, it would be this Sifter Chuck.

"Isss the Winnie Poohs bring top of the dollar," Chuck said. "The Piglets, not so much, the Tiggers, little at all. All Elaki love the Winnie, though. And the storybooks, they read to pouchlings."

David remembered reading the stories in school. He pictured little pouchlings grouped around the Mother-One, and wondered if they identified with Pooh or Christopher Robin.

"Only original versions," Sifter Chuck said. "Bad form to use the Disneys. A pollution, is thought, on home planet."

There were pictures on the wall, of bears made up like old-timey Wanted posters. David gave one a second look. Exactly like the bear that belonged to little Jenny Trey, the one he figured had come to her secondhand, through charity. David moved closer. That was the bear all right.

"Ever see such the bear?" There was a sigh in Sifter Chuck's voice, as if he asked a rhetorical question. "If ever see such a one, please send it my way. Pay you top of the dollar, you must imagine the wealth."

"That valuable?" David said.

"Worth a year of you pay, good sirs, if they pay you well your worth."

David frowned. "You have any like that in stock?"

"No, sirs, this is why the Wanted poster. Nice touch?"

David nodded. "How would I recognize that bear, if I came across one? I mean, how would I know it was the genuine article?"

The Elaki hunched himself together, something like a human shrug. If Sifter Chuck had pockets, his fins would have been tucked inside. "Isss English bear, the Chiltern teddy—short head, wide feet tell you this. Bloodlines British, no doubt. Paw pads velveteen or canvas. But this bear bigger than the usual, and, is softer to touch; like silk this bear's mohair, and the face, for the animal, so sweet. Is called sometimes a Hugmee Bear, for the human sees this and wants to hug. Sifter cocked an eye prong. The Elaki sees this, wants to own. So best to tell, if you see the bear, and desire to hold, to touch, and to have, maybe you have the Chiltern. Values rising, every day. If you know this bear, David Sssilver—"

"No," David said. Too quickly. What was the matter with him today?

"Am always be looking. And for the Pez." The Elaki pointed and David frowned.

"What is that, anyway?"

"Plastic, many colors, a head shape of strange animals, Mickey the Mouse, Animaniacs, Bugging Bunnies."

It looked like a cheap, old-fashioned child's toy. A short plastic cylinder with a silly animal head.

"See, the head props up and a cube of sugar candy emits from the animal neck. Is a wonder, not this? These human children who wish to feed from the neck of cartoon animals? Hard to find, I be telling you, badly made few survive. But worth a fortune to my home buddies. Candy intact would be out of the world."

"If I see one," David said, "I'll be sure and let you know." He brought his ID from his pocket. "I'm a detective, Mr. Sifter, Saigo City Police, Homicide. I'd like to ask you some questions."

Sifter Chuck took a look at the ID, and became still.

"You have come over my young worker human. The Luke Cochran, gone missing these many days?"

"You've seen him?" David asked.

"Not since car go over the ramp, and the uproaring here in this town. We must talk with privacy. Please to follow."

The Elaki moved swiftly when he wanted to, no jittering from side to side. David hesitated. The Elaki turned to one side, stopping at the mouth of a doorway that showed nothing but darkness and shadows.

"Please to come," Sifter Chuck said. His voice was different now, quieter, but firm. The happy-go-lucky salesman was gone.

David followed, feeling nervous. *Too easy*, said the voice in his head. He shrugged and headed toward the Elaki. Even cops got a break now and then.

TWENTY-FIVE

THE HALLWAY WAS DARK, CLOSE, AND HOT, THREE THINGS David did not like. Typical Elaki architecture, he told himself. He wished he had not sent Mel away; he almost wished for Walker.

The hallway twisted and turned, so narrow that David's shoulders brushed both sides. Brian-Smalls would have gotten stuck. David heard music, getting louder the closer they got. The floor sloped upward, the Elaki solution to the staircase problem. The incline got steeper, and then David saw light, and a room that qualified, in an Elaki building, for a second floor. Living space, for Sifter Chuck.

The Elaki looked at him over one shoulder. "Tina Turner."

"What?"

"This music be the Tina Turner. You like to hear the stuff?"

The Elaki pushed a button and the music got louder. David smiled politely and looked around. The floors were a dark linoleum that looked like sheets of hardwood, except, as far as David knew, hardwood did not come in sheets. On the walls were state-of-the-art speakers. Tables, old scarred tables, were covered with bits and pieces of teddy bears, paintbrushes, bottles of chemicals, paint. Bolts of fabric were stacked on a bench.

David lifted an eyebrow.

"Restoration," Sifter Chuck said, and turned the music back down.

The Elaki pulled a battered gold velveteen recliner away from the wall, moved a bag of mohair out of the seat.

"Iss chair for the Cochran, Luke. Please to sit, I know the human gets tired. May I offer you the Elaki coffee?"

David's throat was sore, and he was slightly queasy.

98

Elaki coffee sounded good; it might even settle his stomach.

"Please."

Sifter Chuck slid across the room, working deftly with a pot and some water.

"Iss my Luke Cochran dead?"

"Why do you think he's dead?" David asked.

"You are the cop of the homicide. This means murder, no less."

"What happened that night? The night the car went over the guardrail?"

The Elaki did not answer, seeming to concentrate on the making of the coffee—one thing at a time, very Elaki-like. He did not appear flustered, did not scoot from side to side on his fringe. He moved steadily over the pot, and David smelled fresh ground beans and cinnamon. Elaki coffee, properly made, was the best in the world.

"You have tasted the New Orleans chicory brew?" Sifter Chuck asked companionably.

"No," David said.

"It is interesting, that. With the milk. I would like to make the combination, New Orleans strength, Elaki rich and smoothness, but have yet to make it bind. Am getting close, though."

David closed his eyes for just a moment, lulled. The room was comfortable. He could not remember ever being comfortable in strictly Elaki living space. Oddly enough, he liked the smell of the chemicals, and the polished hardwood, or linoleum, or whatever it was. There was something homey about the disorder, or maybe he was just getting old. Time was when anything out of place made him crazy.

He looked at his watch.

"Patience," the Elaki said. He poured liquid into tiny black cups. "The story I have of the Cochran is something you will like to hear."

David took his coffee from the soft black fin of the Elaki and remembered his father, handing him hot chocolate, while he curled up and watched him work, building the model sailing ships. He realized suddenly why he was comfortable, why he liked the smells, the dust, the disorder of a workshop happily used.

"I am tell you whole story. Leave nothing out."

There was something about Sifter Chuck that made David want to believe that he was going to get the whole story, even though he knew better. The first thing he thought when someone said *I'll tell you everything* was that essentials were being held back. It was a hoop-eared neon ad for "prime yourself, it's a snowjob."

"You wouldn't hold anything back now, would you?" David did not know why he said it. It was bad strategy; he'd just blurted it out to test the waters. God, he felt weird today.

Sifter Chuck rose up on his bottom fringe and gave David a quick, serious look; then he waved a fin, rigid midsection going slack.

"You are policemans official. I hold nothing back."

And then both of them laughed—David out loud, the Elaki, belly rippling. It was impossible for David not to like this guy.

At least they knew where they stood.

The Elaki crumpled sideways, propped against a wide, dusty windowsill, so that he was on eye level with David.

This is for my benefit only, David thought. The Elaki could not be comfortable. He prepared himself to be snowed.

"This young Cochran Luke is the employee for me for many of the months. Work hard, most cheerful, and highly motivated for profit."

"You mean he'd do anything for money?" David said.

"Most anything, this is yes. He not bad inside, not completely. But when it be time for law bending, he is apt and able. This human Luke be the friendly sort, affable. Generous with friends. Too much inclined for the chitchat—typical for the human failing."

"You two do a lot of law bending together, did you?" David asked.

Sifter Chuck twirled a fin, the equivalent of an Elaki shrug. "Is antique business."

"What happened the night Luke disappeared?"

The Elaki refilled David's coffee cup, then settled back in front of the window. "First we must go backward to the groundwork. My Luke is worker boy at university. You know this?"

David nodded, sipping coffee. He felt way too relaxed, almost sleepy. Sunlight came in hot and hard through the window, taking the edge off the chill he'd felt all morning.

"This job pay most well, considering." Sifter Chuck waited.

"Considering what?"

"Nature. Research assistant helper. Go to Elaki family— study on violence. Ask questions the survey."

David frowned. A study on violence? Surveying Elaki?

He didn't feel sleepy anymore. "Why would Elaki answer questions asked by a college junior like Luke Cochran?"

"Isss good this question. Much is the Elaki pridism."

David would have called it racism.

"You might ask me what are the questions on survey."

David felt slow on the uptake. "You really need a straight man here?"

"Please pardon?"

"No, pardon me. Okay, Sifter Chuck. What kind of questions did he ask?"

"Gangs." Sifter hissed, saying the word in the same tone of voice that most people reserved for "tarantula."

Elaki had a terror of human street gangs. An unfounded fear. Gangs were mostly a nasty chapter from the past, relevant as the Devil's Hole Gang was to the 1900's—in other words, history. The Bloods, the Crips, the Chinese Tongs— all had gone into legitimate business in the early years of the twenty-first century when the dinosaurs like IBM and Radio Shack finally rolled over and gave up. They went the route of the Japanese Yakuza, meshing with legitimate business, until trying to separate the two was like trying to pick the nuts out of crunchy peanut butter. They did not want bad press anymore. They had started with group loyalty and some unexpected leadership in the form of Minette

Lydia Kincaid. They left the streets for the profits of the "info" highways, and never looked back. Small, localized gangs would always be a problem, but not like they were before the turn of the century.

"Gangs really aren't a problem these days," David said mildly. "Except in some dug-in enclaves in certain cities, and those are war zones; they don't spill over."

"Have seen the movie," Sifter said.

David sighed. Too many Elaki ideas of Earth came from movies. Earth couldn't export enough of them—or convince the Elaki that what you saw on the screen wasn't necessarily what you got. There were Elaki appreciation groups—read fan clubs—for old-time actors like Mandy Patinkin and the two Elaines, Boosler and Barkin, and for newcomers like Michael Kirk Douglas and the Bombay Boys.

All Elaki had an irrational fear of Earth street gangs, and there was still enough low-level activity from newcomers to feed their fears.

David shook his head. "I can't believe the university would fund research on gangs, not these days."

The Elaki slid sideways on his fringe. "Exactly the point. Why the dog does not bark—isn't there one?"

David put his coffee cup down. "Keep talking."

"Isss like this. Hello, little Elaki Mother-One. I am researcher from Criminology Department, local university. We have to identified all these warning signs of prediction victims. And from answers here, sorry to inform but it looks like next victim be you."

David put his coffee cup down.

Sifter Chuck cocked an eye prong. "Gets this now, you do? For a sum of the cash, can let this family know how not to become the victim of."

"You're saying this kid was running an extortion racket?" David thought of Cochran's mother, evasive about Luke's money, but refusing to take cash or gifts. She'd said it was because he needed the money. But a kid with a car like a Visck wasn't hurting. Maybe this was the case of an honest woman who wouldn't turn her son in but wanted no part of his dirty money.

"Not alone, him," the Elaki said.

David looked up. "What?"

"Him just the risk man. Is run by university professor. You don't believe?"

"How does this bring us to a blood sanction in Elaki-Town?"

"These Elaki they survey and pay up or not. But if pay up, do expect the protection to be. And a young female pouchling, also the student of university, gets a gangland gun-down after the pay up big time."

"You're talking about the Race Street shooting."

"Yes, this be the one."

David nodded slowly. That one had rippled far and wide, but never a hint of the extortion angle. From what he remembered, the Elaki Mother-One and the victims pouch-sib had been completely uncooperative with the police—business as usual.

They'd deal with it on their own. And it looked like they had.

"So he's dead, then," David said. He thought of Miriam. He was glad Mel wasn't around.

"Not dead," the Elaki said. "All is background this. Now for unfolding night events."

Story time, David thought, settling back. This was where the Elaki would get tricky.

"Three are sent for the fetch. There is much talk of blood sanction. This is not function of Izicho, so is community business. Must have unanimous quorum for blood sanction, and is much personal risk. Izicho do not like community sanction—for to hog power unto selves. So if displeased, could be concussion. This is the word?"

"Repercussion, I think you mean."

"Ah, yes this. Also, do not wish human law troubles. Elaki-Town is commerce center, no wealthy no worker Elaki privilege lazy behinders. Work here for living, all human almighty dollar provinces. Blend well, we thinks."

Nothing much about Elaki-Town suggested blending, but David did not comment.

"And big trouble much, because of the woman."

David sat forward. "What happened to the woman?"

"Much is the mystery."

"What do you mean?" David could not keep his foot still.

"She there, then she gone. Disappear. No one knows. Could be some know and don't talk. She is the innocent in the clear, and much is made of her involvement. She be witness, not legitimate to kill. If she is to die, this be bad act, open to moral sanction anybody's direction. If not, she will know Luke's fate. This, plus my own pitch of talk talk intervention is the savior of Luke Cochran. And maybe of her."

"You telling me Cochran survived?"

"Yes. Is rioting swarm, and deep is the fear. Very many Elaki, milling in streets that have been made dark. All with the many opinions. But victim gang shoot most popular, valued female. This also to down-and-out Elaki-Town. Bad victim choice for the ultimate survival, Luke Cochran. Is riotous mass, and difficult to be heard. So even though he is talked clear by me myself, also must escort personally out."

"Doesn't seem possible," David said.

"No. The backs will turn, not to witness the shame of him, unpunished for murder or the crime betrayal. So go then and go quickly, and do not see the woman again. But damn sure the Cochran is to be the safe escort out of the Elaki-Town. He goes and goes fast. He be okay. I know this."

"Then where is he now?" David said.

"I wish to be first to know."

David sighed. He knew the feeling.

TWENTY-SIX

DAVID DECIDED TO GO ON THE OFFENSIVE WITH THE UNIversity professors. One, they'd have been waiting for a knock on their door since Cochran disappeared, so they were going to be in a sweat; two, they hadn't volunteered any information, so they were covering their asses; and three, his prejudices told him that they'd be a precious pain, up on their dignity, and arrogant.

And he had no time to waste.

There were two of them—the female, a full professor of psychology with a minor degree in criminology, and the male, an associate who was Cochran's advisor, and part of the research project that had employed Luke Cochran on work-study. He'd seen them both in the hallway, and something about the woman had rung his bell—cop vibes, whatever you wanted to call it. He'd learned to treat those feelings with respect.

For that reason alone, he considered letting someone else take her on. He didn't like her. He was going to have an attitude. But instead he sent String and Mel across the hall with the guy, and set Dr. Dunkirk aside for himself.

David took a last sip of cold coffee, watched Della approach his desk.

"How's she doing?" he asked.

Della shook her head. "I don't think she's cooking, David. I don't think she cares. She took the smokes, and the sandwich, passed on the bathroom—which you know they never do if they're *at all* nervous. Asked me for a note pad, and last I looked, she's sitting in there making notes for her next lecture. You could leave her all night, I don't think it'll accomplish a thing."

David nodded. A tough one, and he wasn't surprised. He'd felt like hell when he'd come in, but a rush of adrenaline had him looking forward to this.

He wiped his palms on the knees of his pants. "What about the guy?"

Della grinned. "Mel and String got him cornered. They don't be careful, he's going to go mute. He sure sweats a lot, for a college professor."

"What was his name again?"

"Albee. Dr. Kirkland Albee."

"Okay. Set up the holographer and the Miranda Pro, and I'll be right in."

"You going to scare even this lady, you keep that grim look on your face. You feeling bad?"

He nodded.

"Use it, baby. You want some aspirin, let me know."

"I got Tylenol Twelve in my desk."

"Hell, David, that wussy stuff ain't no good. You really hurting, let me give you some of those Platinum Advils. Your body will feel better three minutes after you suck those babies down. I also got an Excedrin Inhaler. Works fast, but doesn't last as long."

David shook his head and waved her off. If he didn't feel better after the interview, he would take all three at once. He rummaged in his desk for the Tylenol.

Professor Dunkirk was all smiles when David walked into the room on the heels of the technical setup. Which was damning, David thought. She ought to be pissed. Her good-natured cheerfulness was a definite misstep.

Error number one, David thought, and felt better. He reminded himself that the woman might be innocent.

But he looked in her face and knew better.

"I'm Detective Silver, Homicide."

She kept smiling, outwardly unfazed by the homicide tag. Weird weird weird.

"I have to tell you, Detective, I have a degree in criminology, and I'm actually pretty excited about being interviewed. Gives me a chance for some first-hand observation."

David sat down. "The first thing I'm going to do is advise you of your rights."

"The woman already did that."

Voice a bit testy, David thought. He looked at her a long moment. Checked the machine. "Good."

She frowned. Stared at him. She was a plain woman, big-boned and self-confident. Her hair was thick, dark brown, held back in an unsophisticated ponytail by a red rubber band. She wore khaki trousers, and a flannel shirt with a white T-shirt underneath, even though the outside temperature was in the upper eighties. Her shoes were heavy lace-ups. Her complexion was ruddy, skin rough and patchy. Eyelashes pale, no makeup.

She would look at home behind a tractor, or on a loading dock.

She raised a square, callused hand. "I'm doing my best to cooperate here. I've studied police work, police methods." She grinned—strong, white teeth. "I'm on your side, Detective, okay?"

It was gentle, but she was chastening him. He looked at her coldly.

"I've got enough on you for obstruction of justice, easily, so you're definitely going to be held."

"Obstruction of—"

"It's a b.s. thing, as you likely know. But we'll keep you with it till the DA decides what level of homicide to go with. Where we move from there depends a lot on how much you tell me, how much help you can be."

Her mouth hung open, and David could see a clot of spittle at the edges.

"*What* are you talking about? Are you sure you don't have me mixed up with somebody else?"

He glanced at his notes, though there was no need. "Professor Elizabeth Dunkirk, Saigo City University, teaching and research position."

"But what is all this about?"

David gave her steady look. "It's about Luke Cochran, Dr. Dunkirk, and you've already wasted five minutes of my time with your posturing." He shifted sideways. Somewhere in the back of his mind he knew his body ached and moaned, but he felt good. He was going to get his teeth into this one.

He lifted a hand. Languidly. "I'll tell you the truth. I think you're a waste of time, and it's time I don't have. I'm in the middle of a murder investigation, and I've got a missing person. Looks like we'll have more luck with your friend next door, and that's good enough for me. You want your paralegal, I'll put the word out, and we'll put an end to our little session right now."

Her eyes went wide; her feelings were hurt. He looked at her hands, which were steady. Interesting. They should have been shaking—anger, fear, something. He was giving her the rough end; she ought to be upset. Her words said "upset," but her body did not.

Formidable, this one.

"You haven't even told me what this is about."

She was toying with him. David felt a spurt of admiration. Decided to turn up the heat.

He slammed a hand hard on the tabletop. "See? You're doing it. Stalling, playing dumb. I don't feel good, I'll be honest with you. I'm sick as a dog. I don't have the—"

"Luke was sick, too."

David settled back in his chair. "What?"

"I said Luke was sick, too. That's what this is about, isn't it? Luke Cochran?"

David stared at her.

"Is he dead?" she asked.

"Where'd you hide the body?" David asked back.

She gasped. *"What?"*

"The *body*. His mortal remains."

"I didn't kill him."

"We know all about the extortion scam. We know it blew up in your face."

She folded her arms.

"We know he came to you for help, and you turned your back." A shot in the dark, but it hit home, he could tell. He was getting to her, finally. "I don't blame you for being scared. Elaki blood sanctions are a death sentence, and not a very nice one. I'll feel sorry for you when this hits the papers.'' She flinched. ''But Luke Cochran was a twenty-year-old college kid.''

''If he had a sanction out on him, and I'm not saying he did, why would I bother to kill him? Makes no sense, Detective.''

''But it does, *Dr.* Dunkirk. If the Elaki get hold of him, he'll talk. He'll mention *your* name. It's only human, right? He'll give them you, to try and save himself. And you're still walking around and he's gone. If the Elaki got him, they'd have you too—you're a bigger prize. In my book, your very presence in this room means you did it.''

''I *did not* kill Luke Cochran.'' There was a coating of sweat on her upper lip and she licked it clean with a beefy red tongue. David felt his stomach churn.

''Fine,'' he said. He stood up and headed for the door. He actually had it open—he was moving quickly—when she broke.

''You let this hit the media, you'll get me sanctioned for sure, Detective.''

David caught sight of Della in the hallway. She winked, held up the Excedrin Inhalant.

His head was pounding, he wished he could have the inhalant, but he was playing the big scene here, and had to let it go.

He shut the door and leaned his back into the knob. ''I really don't care.''

She looked at him.

''Speaking objectively, if I were you, I'd remain in police custody. That won't be hard, because you're going to be charged. And the Elaki may have forgotten you, by the time you get out, because I'm not stopping with the murder of Cochran; I'm looking into that Elaki student who got killed, in spite of the protection money her Mother-One paid up.'' He stuck a thumb in his belt loop. ''Come to think of it, I guess you're right. You may be breathing, right at the moment, but you're probably dead.''

''I *did not kill* Luke Cochran. I *did not* have anything to do with the death of that Elaki kid; it was a bad coincidence.''

''I'll say.''

''Look, I'm not stupid. I know you can keep this out of the media, or at least see my side gets told. I know you can.''

David folded his arms. Looked at her. She was bent almost double in her chair, leaning toward him, hands out.

''Give me a reason,'' David said coldly.

She sat back. Took a deep breath. ''First off, I didn't kill anybody. The student who got shot was killed by the gang thing. It was a holdup really; she was down on Race Street, for crissake. I guess . . . I guess she felt safe.''

''Her Mother-One paid protection money. They thought they were protected.''

''It was a risk factor I never even thought of.'' Her voice had dropped; she was almost conversational.

David shook his head. ''Easy money, right, Beth? Elaki are terrified of gangs, they watch all those old Spike Lee movies. So you go play on that fear, in the guise of a survey. Find out their habits, analyze their risk factors, and lo and behold, the magic computer program predicts with a ninety-nine percent probability that they're going to be a victim.''

''Eighty-nine.''

''What?''

''Eighty-nine percent probability.''

''And then what?''

''Then they pay our expense money and we tell them exactly what they need to do to alter the risk factor and stay safe.''

''And since Elaki don't trust their own police, much less ours, nobody complains.''

She shrugged. ''We only hit them once, and then it's over.''

''Not for the family of this female student.''

Her eyes went dull. ''We forgot the stupidity factor.''

David scratched his chin, realized he'd forgotten to

shave. The rasping noise seemed to bother her, so he kept doing it.

"Once I walk through that door there, Beth, this conversation is over and you'll be alive at five. If that's not what you want, you better talk to me now, and you better talk to me fast, and you better tell me things I want to hear."

"I don't think Luke got sanctioned at all. You find a body?"

David said nothing.

"Because he had friends over there in Elaki-Town. Did you know about his job with that antique dealer, Sifter?"

"Yeah."

"I'll bet there's things about that job you don't know." Smug, this.

"I'm listening." David made a point of not looking impressed, but inwardly he smiled. It was a nice cross-ruff he had going. Sifter Chuck was happy to tell him everything about the university scam to draw attention from his own involvement, and vice versa. The main complication was deciding which of them had Luke. And where the hell Miriam was.

Dunkirk leaned sideways, one elbow on the table. "They were faking antiques, manufacturing them on the home planet, then bringing them down here. Luke hid them, made the plants, so they could be discovered one by one over the next few years."

"What antiques were they faking?"

"Teddy bears, believe it or not."

David believed it. "I don't see anything here that would get him killed. Nothing that would cause a blood sanction. The best murder motive still involves you, Elizabeth."

"Think so? Because my experience is that revenge; hell, everything always takes a back seat to money."

David kept quiet, but he didn't disagree.

"He pinched one of the bears," Dunkirk said. "Gave it to his girlfriend for her kids. Those bears are worth a fortune to the Elaki, plus there's always the question of where she got it. So not only did Luke cost this Sifter a big hunk of money, but he endangered the whole operation."

"How'd you find out about all this?"

She shrugged. Touched the package of cigarettes, but didn't take one. "He was talky, Luke was. He was young; okay, guys that age always want to talk about it. Actually, he asked my advice. He decided he better get that bear away from his girlfriend, but he didn't want to let her know what was going on. Seemed to me he'd have been better off just telling her flat-out, but he was very touchy about that part. Said she absolutely could not know it was a fake, manufactured off-planet. And he was getting sick. He'd get better, then worse. So he was getting hard to deal with."

"What was wrong with him?"

"I'm not sure. First they thought it was the flu. Then it was some kind of mono, or walking pneumonia. Then a virus."

"He was seeing a doctor?"

"Going to Student Health. Tell you the truth, I advised him to go to a real doctor. I think he tried, but the waiting lists were unreal, and he didn't have any kind of clout. They told him he was stuck with Student Health. Which, believe me, Detective, is stuck."

"Luke ever mention a Miriam Kellog?"

Dunkirk made a face. Nodded slowly. "He mentioned the name; I just don't remember the context. I think she may have been the baby's doctor. The one who died."

"How did Luke take it?"

"The baby dying? Kind of weird. I always suspected the kid was his. He seemed stunned, and kind of worried. Anxious, like. And he definitely did not like this Miriam woman. Said she was pushy."

"Did he ever admit he was the baby's father?"

She shrugged. "He never came out and said it. It was just the way he talked about the kid. Kind of proud. And he took both of the kids toys sometimes. Tried to give his girlfriend money."

"Tried?"

"Kind of pissed him off, as I recall. Cause she never would take it."

TWENTY-SEVEN

THE LAST PERSON DAVID EXPECTED TO SEE IN THE HOMIcide bullpen was his daughter Kendra. As soon as she saw him, she swallowed hard, turned her head to one side.

"Uncle Mel wouldn't mind me sitting at his desk," she said quickly, chin jutting.

David wondered how their relationship had gotten so adversarial. He perched on the edge of the desk, leg swinging. "Everything okay at home?"

She shrugged. He was aware of the benevolent interest of his coworkers, grateful that they went about their business as if nothing was amiss. Why, he thought, was it such an aberration for a child to visit the bullpen? A lot of the detectives had kids, but you never saw them anywhere but at the annual picnic.

Someone had put three candy bars, two Cokes, and one Dr. Pepper on the desk, next to the phone. David felt a rush of gratitude to whoever had provided the goodies. Della most likely.

"Sisters around?" David asked mildly.

Kendra's bottom lip quivered.

David leaned toward her. "What's the matter, Kendra? Tell me."

She pulled away. "I know you're going to be mad, so yell at *me*, okay? Because this was my idea."

David looked at her. "Is your mother all right?"

Kendra looked guilty, gave him an impatient look.

"She know you're here?" he asked.

Kendra shook her head. "She had to go out. But she called to see if we were okay. I told her about Pid, but she said to let her worry about it when she got home for supper. She said for us to do our homework and clean our rooms, and not to bother you. But you're our dad, aren't you?"

David nodded, wary here. "How'd you get down here, Kendra?"

She gripped the edge of the desk. "We took the SART."

David opened his mouth. Closed it. "You took the transit? You took SART?"

Kendra nodded and blinked back tears. "I watched both of them the whole way—"

"Both . . . Lisa and Mattie? You took Mattie on SART?"

"I held her hand and we took the long route, so we wouldn't go anywhere near Little Saigo."

People were staring. No doubt, David thought, he had turned chalk-white. He felt chalk-white.

"You know better." He was aware of the ominous parental overtone in his voice. "Where are your sisters?"

"In the bathroom."

"But they're here?"

"Yes. Yes, sir."

David took a breath. "So all of you are okay, or you will be until I kill you?"

"Daddy, we didn't have enough money for cab fare all the way in from the house! We were afraid he was going to die. We tried to feed him milk and sugar, just like you showed us, but he wouldn't eat no matter what."

David was afraid to ask. He closed his eyes. He? Surely not. He heard a shriek and a squeal and he recognized the distressed and excited voice of his youngest. He hesitated. He did not want to look.

The piglet ran across the floor, small legs pumping. More of a hop than a run, slow but frantic. Mattie and Lisa were right behind him, hot and sweaty, clothes wrinkled and stained, hair windblown and tangled.

"You guys rode the SART with a pig?"

"*Daddy.*" Mattie ran and grabbed his knees, turned her small face up to look at him. "We put him in a backpack, but he wouldn't stay. He wouldn't be still."

The pig made it to David's feet and collapsed on his shoes.

Lisa looked at him from across the room. "I'm afraid he

made a mess in the bathroom, Daddy.'' Somewhere behind him, David heard snickers, a giggle. Lisa put her hands behind her back. ''I cleaned it up as best as I could.''

The laughter stopped suddenly. The room got quiet.

''Something going on I should know about?''

David recognized the voice of Captain Halliday. He turned around slowly.

''Uh, Captain—''

''David? Is that a—'' Halliday's frown cleared when he spotted the girls. ''Hi, kids. Mattie. Lisa. Kendra, when did you grow up?''

David's daughters smiled politely, little faces tight and worried.

''Is it take-your-daughter-to-work-day again already?''

Lisa shook her head. ''No, sir.''

''It's take-your-pig-to-work-day,'' someone said. David wasn't sure who.

Halliday moved close to David, pointed chin dropping to his chest. He was wearing suspenders every day now, and as usual, they sagged off the narrow, sloping shoulders.

''Is Rose around?''

''No, no she's not.'' David shook his head for emphasis. Halliday did not like Rose.''

''I see. But, isn't that a—''

''Livestock!''

The shriek made Mattie frown and tear up. Walker waved a fin and skittered toward Pid.

''A pig in the—''

Halliday turned, his face going dark, corners of his mouth tight. ''Walker. A little decorum, please; you're upsetting the children.''

''Pouchlings and pigs in bullpen?''

Kendra moved in front of Mattie. ''It's not a bullpen now, it's a—''

''Don't say it,'' David told her quietly. She glared at him.

''Pigpen!'' Walker said. ''This is the unprofessional worst.''

Halliday went stiff. ''Quit waving your flippers there at

those children. You don't have little ones in your home
place, Walker?"

"No pouchlings in office."

"You got pigs," someone muttered. "Of a sort."

Halliday put a hand on one hip. "We're *human* here,
Walker, most of us anyway. That means we can be flexible.
David?"

Get rid of the pig, David thought.

Halliday nodded at him. "When you get your, um, do-
mestic crisis resolved, I'd like an update."

"Yes, sir."

Halliday gave him a nod and headed for the glass cubicle
he called home.

Walker emitted a whistling sigh, rocked back on her bottom fringe, and cocked one eye prong at David. "That
works well. You thank me now."

"What?"

"He was to blow the sky till I come in the offender.
Humans all stick together, so predictable."

David lifted Pid up off the floor. "You want to pet
him?"

"No need. One Earth creature of a much like another."
Walker rolled away, leaving a trail of flaking scales.

"Go and molt yourself," David muttered.

"I hear this, Detective David Silver, sirs. Some big thank
you much."

TWENTY-EIGHT

LISA, KENDRA, AND MATTIE STOOD IN A HORSESHOE around David's chair, watching anxiously as Pid lapped milk from David's coffee cup.

"He wants more," Mattie said.

The pig looked up and snuffled the can of Coke, nudging it close to the edge of the desk. The girls looked at David, a question in their eyes. David shrugged and poured Coke into the mug. Pid took a small, timid taste, then began lapping the sweet fizzy brown liquid.

"He likes it!" Lisa said.

Della leaned over the back of David's chair. "I'll be darned. A Coke-swilling pig. What will they think of next, those Silvers?"

David looked at her. "I won't make the obvious comment."

She hoisted her ever-ready can of Coke. "Not if you value your life, you won't."

The phone rang. David looked for Della, his arms full of pig. Wondered where had she gotten to in such a hurry.

"I'll get it, Daddy." Kendra picked up the receiver, cleared her throat. "Homicide, Silver. What? *Castrated?* It's me, Uncle Mel. Yeah, I'll forget what you said." She glanced at David. "No, Daddy didn't hear you. Can I take a message or do you need to talk to Dad? Oh. Feeding a pig."

David groaned.

"What? Yeah, I'll tell him. Huh?" Her eyes squinched tighter. "Okay. Okay. Yeah, I got it. Okay. Yeah. Okay."

"Let me talk to him," David said.

Kendra hung up. "Uncle Mel has a message for you, Daddy."

"So I gathered."

"He says . . . Now what was it?"

"*Kendra.*"

"Just kidding. Him and String talked to some doctor at that hospital."

"Which hospital?"

Kendra frowned. "He didn't say. He just told me that the hospital guy said they didn't suspect the mother, and it wasn't them that started the circus."

David felt Pid lick his fingers. "Anything else?"

"Yeah, it was the social worker who blew the whistle. Uncle Mel called her office but she went home early. You want to meet him over at her house?"

"Yeah," David said.

Kendra nodded. "Good. That's what I told him."

"I don't suppose you got the address?"

"Eighteen-oh-four Mercer. Be there in forty minutes. And don't worry about us, Daddy. We can go back on the SART, I know what I'm doing."

David pointed a finger at her. "No, you will not. *Ever* again. That clear?"

"Yes, sir."

"Yes, sir."

"Yes, sir."

"Yes, sir."

David glanced around the room, wondering where that fourth "yes, sir" had come from. The pig licked his fingers and moved up his wrist, nuzzling his shirt sleeve. He glanced at his watch, which was sticky.

"No time to take you ladies home, so I guess I'll have to make you deputies."

Mattie touched the piglet's soft pink ear. "Can Pid be a deputy too?"

Della looked at them over the top of her terminal. "No problem, girlfriend. Let me get that sucker a badge."

TWENTY-NINE

DAVID SETTLED THE GIRLS UNDER A SHADY TREE IN A TINY park catty-corner to Angie Nassif's duplex. Mel crossed the road tracks, waving at the girls.

David looked at him. "Meet my deputies."

"The pig too?" Mel asked.

"He's got a badge," Lisa said.

"Get out of here."

"Yep, Della give it to him." Mattie put her arms out and Mel swooped her up. She gave him a sticky kiss. "We dropped in on Daddy at the office. We took Pid."

"Yeah? How'd you kiddos get downtown?" He looked sideways at Kendra. "Or are you driving now?"

"No. I brought us in on the SART."

"You kidding?" He raised an eyebrow. "You ever wonder what they call the rapid transit system down in Florida?"

David put a hand over Kendra's mouth. "No, Mel, she doesn't."

Angie Nassif's door sensor picked them up before they made the top porch step.

"Please state your name and business."

"Detectives Silver and Burnett." David held his ID up to be scanned, glanced back at the girls.

It was a good enough neighborhood. They should be okay out of the sun and under the tree. In his mind's eye, they sat together, talking and laughing softly, discussing literature. In reality they were fighting.

David sighed, raised his voice. "Lisa, Kendra!"

They looked up.

"Quit playing accordion with your sister." David looked at Mel, wondering if he should voice his conclusions about

Miriam. "You ever thought about having some of your own, Mel?"

"Some what?"

The door was opened by a waif with long blond hair and ears that stuck out. She wore a T-shirt three sizes too big, and loose, boxy cotton shorts, as if she were hiding behind her clothes. Her heavy, high-top boots were untied, the laces loose and sloppy, though the current look was buttoned-up. Her hair was parted in the middle, and it hung heavily in her face. She brushed it out of her eyes and shifted her weight to her left foot.

David saw rubbery red scars crisscrossing one slender wrist.

"Can I help you?"

Her voice was so soft, David found himself leaning forward to hear. "Detectives Silver and Burnett, here to see Angie Nassif."

"Please come in." The girl stood back, head bowed.

David caught her peeping up at him and he smiled.

She ducked her head.

"Angie's in the middle of her workout, but you can come on back." She waved a hand that was shaking.

David wondered if she was always this nervous. He kept his voice gentle. "I don't think I caught *your* name."

"Crystal," she said, as if it were a shame.

It embarrassed David when they trooped in behind Crystal and caught Angie Nassif in tight pink shorts and halter bra. She was built like a fireplug, arms muscular, slick with sweat as she lifted the barbell. David wondered how many pounds the end weights came to.

More than he could lift, no doubt.

Angie did a double take when she saw them, and irritation emanated from her like an electric current. She set the weights down carefully, pulled the pink bandanna off her head and wiped her cleavage.

David looked away.

"You guys aware I have an office?"

Crystal took a step backward. "They said they were

homicide police, Angie; they probably want to talk to you about—''

David looked up, interested, but Angie waved a hand curtly, cutting the girl off.

''That's okay, Crystal. Why don't we all sit down?''

Mel took the red plaid couch, David the matching chair. The furniture was expensive, new, bland. Shades of deep red and hard blue, a combination David did not find soothing.

Nassif sat in a Bentwood rocker, the only thing in the room David did like. She laid her palms on her bare knees.

''So. What's this all about?''

''Annie Trey. And her baby,'' Mel said.

David watched Crystal. She had stayed on her feet and folded her arms. She leaned against the sliding glass door in a position that should have looked relaxed, but didn't.

''What about them?''

Mel leaned back against the couch, crossed one leg. ''I've seen you on the news and stuff. Very evenhanded, careful not to presume innocence or guilt.''

Nassif nodded as if this were a tune she'd heard before. ''That's the job description, fellas.'' She smiled tolerantly in a way that made David want to smack her.

''How'd the investigation get started up, anyway? Who brought you in?'' David asked.

Nassif waved a hand. ''Routine hospital inquiry.''

David watched Crystal out of the corner of his eye, saw her fold her arms tighter and wedge herself against the glass. Nassif saw him watching, gave Crystal a look. The girl turned her back on them, peered outdoors.

''I don't think so,'' David said.

Nassif smiled pleasantly. ''Pardon?''

Mel scratched the side of his nose. ''He means you're lying to us and we're calling you on it.''

Nassif sat forward. ''Gee, thanks for the translation, Detective. Now look, guys. I deal with assholes like you two every day of my life. It's all part of the crusade, so don't think you're rattling me. I get tired of men like you. Guys who don't believe bad things happen in good families, judges who—''

''There are three little girls across the street in the park playing with a baby pig,'' Crystal said, blinking and smiling shyly at Nassif and the detectives, as if she had not heard any of their conversation, or been aware they were having one.

''Piglet, Crystal,'' Nassif said.

''What?''

''A baby pig is a piglet.''

She would always have to be right, David realized. Angie Nassif would have rules of behavior for everyone, and a solid, ingrained conviction that she knew what was best and let the chips fall. Definitely one of the scariest women he'd ever met.

''Crystal. Why don't you go see if the girls will let you pet the baby pig?''

It was an order, but Crystal smiled at Angie Nassif like she'd been offered a treat. She slid the door open, careful to close it behind her.

''Piglet,'' Mel said.

Nassif blinked. ''What?''

''A baby pig is a piglet.''

''What a funny guy. Did the two of you just stop by to make me laugh? Because I think you're out of line, coming to my home like this.''

Mel wagged a finger at her. ''Now, Angie, if you hadn't been a naughty girl and sneaked home early, we wouldn't have to be here in the middle of your red plaid couch. Who does your decorating, anyway?''

She took a hard, short breath. ''You're Burnett, right?''

''Two t's,'' Mel said.

David did not like the look in her eyes. ''Who put you on this, Ms. Nassif? Who called it in?''

She would not meet his eyes. ''You can't ask me that. It's confidential. Anonymous source.''

''Not in an ongoing homicide investigation.''

''Did you find Luke's—'' She stopped.

Mel raised an eyebrow. ''Body? No. But we got a bloody

tennis shoe, you want to drop in and look at it, and no sign yet of the kid.''

Nassif bit her lip. "What's Annie got to do with this?"

"You know Miriam Kellog?" David asked.

Nassif's lips formed a tight, straight line. "I've met the woman. An *expert* forensic scientist."

David knew without looking that Mel was ready to blow. "What was the problem between you?"

Nassif shrugged. "No problem."

"She riding you?" Mel asked. "Maybe she was wondering why you're having Annie Trey crucified in the press. Maybe she was wondering what started you pointing a finger and running around in circles yelling 'poison.' "

Nassif shook a finger at them. "You know if I *didn't* do anything, and the other child came up dead, you'd be screaming negligence. I got a job to do and I do it."

David leaned forward. "Who, Ms. Nassif? Who made the complaint?"

She shook her head. "Not going to happen. Not going to tell you."

"I'll have your records subpoenaed."

"Best of luck, Detective. In the meantime, how's *your* home life? You got kids of your own?"

The anger was so sudden and so intense that for a moment David could not breathe. And laced with the anger was a sliver of fear. How was his home life? Okay, except his wife threw things at him whenever he walked through the door. Perfect environment for nurturing children.

Mel leaned forward. "Hey, lady, you late for your medication or something?"

Nassif stuck her chin up. "Everybody's vulnerable to Social Services."

Mel leaned back against the couch, stretching his arm along the top. He smiled. "So true, Angie girlfriend. And Crystal there looks underage to me."

Nassif flushed a thick dusky red that crept from the top of her halter bra, up her neck, across her cheeks. "That girl has been victimized all her life, victimized by men just like you. My home is a *haven* for her."

"No doubt you make beautiful music, blah blah blah, so what? My partner here happens to be a world-class father, so don't give yourself airs. 'Cause you mess with him, and that'll piss me off." He leaned forward, voice going low. "And believe me, you don't know from victimized."

"You guys get out."

David stood up. "I'll have a court order ready in twenty-four hours. Watch for it."

"Have somebody read it to you," Mel said.

THIRTY

THERE WERE NO RESTAURANTS THAT ALLOWED PIGS IN THE dining room in any capacity other than barbecue, and it was too hot to leave Pid in the car, which was why they ended up eating at the Thunderboat. The kids loved eating there, and though he complained about the food, David liked it too, grease and all. It was a period piece, shaped like a sailboat, blue paint peeling. The hook was car speakers that fit in your windows, and human employees who brought food on a tray that clamped to your door.

There were picnic tables and a playground, a scummy fish pond, and a sandpit for pouchlings where the girls put Pid while they ate. The pig was feeling energetic, and tried to climb the sides of the pit three times, each time sliding back down to the bottom. He finally curled up and went to sleep.

The girls sat at a table near Pid, and David sat farther away, across from Mel, String, and Aslanti. Aslanti was part of String's chemaki—the Elaki family grouping String had formed to meet the needs of the human child he had co-adopted with another Elaki police officer. The child was the son of Arson Investigator Yolanda Free Clements, who had died in the line of duty, and left the care of her son to her Elaki partner, another member of the chemaki.

One thing that David loved about the Thunderboat was that it only catered to humans. Elaki were welcome, there was a sandpit for the pouchlings after all, but there was no cinnamon in the food and no tacos on the menu.

String licked the straw in his root beer float.

Mel shook his head. "You don't lick it, String, you suck it. Haven't you figured out straws?"

"The ice cream bobs and will not be still."

"That's why it's called a 'float,' so it's not like you weren't warned."

David unwrapped the double-wide cheeseburger with catsup, mayonnaise, onion, lettuce, tomato, and pickle. It had almost sounded good, thirty minutes ago. He looked at a grease spot on the table. A dead fly had died happily in the middle.

Mel crunched an onion ring. "So then I say, 'Hey, that girl of yours, Crystal, looks like she's underage to me.' "

Aslanti took a bite of chicken salad on whole wheat. "Must take care with these workers who are social."

David rewrapped the burger, shivered, looked at Mel. "You forgot the part where you asked her if she was late for her meds."

String quit eating and David saw his belly ripple. Elaki amusement.

Mel looked at David. "You can't be cold."

Aslanti swiveled an eye prong in his direction. "Outdoor temperature still in the eight zeros now, even as the sun packs up."

Mel wiped his fingers on a napkin. "You don't look good, David. You sick or something?"

"Tired." David took a sip of iced tea. It felt good going down his throat.

"You're pale, you know that? And you're sweating."

"You're sweating too," David said.

"Yeah, but I'm not shaking."

David turned to look at his daughters. Mattie was feeding Pid the end of her chili dog. Sometime during this long day the pig had crossed a threshold, and was eating almost everything in sight. Lisa wore her disc phones, eyes dreamy, tuned out. She nodded her head to music only she could hear, and divided her barbecue into tiny little pieces, then chewed them slowly, one by one.

David was glad, suddenly, that his daughters were with him. He was convinced that Annie Trey had not hurt her infant son. He promised himself that somehow, in the course of the investigation, he'd clear her name. Some days he liked his work.

He looked at the car. The drive home was going to be long and grueling. He promised himself early bed.

He thought of Crystal, how she had happily been stroking Pid's soft white flank when he and Mel came out of the house. She seemed quite comfortable with his daughters, but as soon as she saw David and Mel, she'd headed back across the street. She had a peculiar walk, a kind of sideways shuffle where she stared at the ground, then lifted her head in a quick, furtive reconnaissance before tilting it sideways, and staring back down.

David watched that walk and would have known, even without Nassif's backfill, that Crystal had the kind of background he didn't want to know about.

He looked up, realized Mel was watching him.

"Welcome to the world, David."

"I'm sorry, what?"

"Aslanti wants access to some of the physical samples Miriam took during the baby's autopsy."

David looked at the her. "You've seen Miriam's notes?"

"String bring them. Some bits of true interest. Would like to run a simple test, maybe three. Even four."

David frowned. "I doubt we can get you access."

Mel quit chewing. "What about that Caper guy, Sam? He seemed okay; maybe he could run them for her."

"Yesss," String said. "Runs tests under wing span homicide."

"Something like that," Mel said.

David nodded. "Worth a try." He was tired of craning his neck to look up at the Elaki. He put his cheeseburger back in the bag. Maybe one of the kids would eat it on the way home. "Okay, guys, I'm going to call it a night. You going home, Mel, or coming with me?"

"No offense, David, but peace and quiet sound attractive tonight."

"Must not be coming to my house." He turned away, heard Aslanti say "please to excuse," heard her sliding along the pavement behind him.

He glanced backward, gave her a lopsided smile. "You want me?"

She kept rolling, moving along at a good clip. David saw Mel give them a look.

"Progress further into the parking lake for to get privacy."

"Lot," David said.

"What?"

"Parking lot."

She looked at him, a look that gave him pause. He followed her, hands in pockets. She stopped by an empty speaker, and David leaned against the white metal support post. His back scraped shreds of paint and he knew they would cling to his shirt. He was too tired to care. He held his jacket, sweaty palms making wrinkles in the khaki sleeves.

"What's up," David said.

"You have had much time spent with this Trey, Annie?"

David scratched his neck. "Some. If you want my opinion, I think she's innocent."

"And she has other children?"

"A little girl. Jenny. Eighteen months old, give or take."

"Girl for sure, no boys child? Other than sad infant mortality?"

David swallowed, tried not to think about how sore his throat felt. It was the heat, that was all. This heat would take it out of anybody.

"And you, Silver David? These three noise happy ones are yours?"

"All mine."

"Are there more? Male ones?" Both of Aslanti's eye prongs were slanted his way, and layered beneath the Elaki nonchalance was a concern that made him wipe the sweat from his upper lip.

"No. No boys."

"Good this is."

The normal thing to do would be to ask her why—why did it matter if he'd spent time with Annie Trey, if either of them had male children? Her newborn baby had been male, and her newborn baby was dead. If the child hadn't been poisoned, what had killed him?

Something extremely toxic, according to the autopsy. Something swift and nasty.

Oddly enough, he was not curious. He just wanted to take his girls and his pig and go home. He tried to smile.

"We appreciate your time and trouble, Aslanti. It's late, though. Time I got my girls home and in bed."

"Detective David, pleasss. How physical do you be feeling?"

"Listen, Aslanti, don't go all medical on me. Learn to leave your work at the office."

"My work is how I finds me. Please answer."

David shrugged. "Fine. I feel fine."

"Do not looks fine."

"I'm a little tired, that's all."

"Throat sore? Hot the cold sweats, panic tight in the chest?"

David's mouth went dry. "No. Yes." He ran a hand through his hair. "Okay, maybe a little, but not that much."

She skittered sideways. "Blood, please."

"What?"

"Quick sample souvenir." She had that tension in her belly that let him know she was attempting a joke.

He felt strange following her to her van—as if he were walking on the bottom of the ocean. He looked at String and Mel, deep in conversation. They did not notice Aslanti take out a thin blue case, reach for the packet of latent nano retrievers. She opened a small laptop, about the size of a sandwich, spoke to it softly, emptied the packet into an opening at the top.

She scuttled close and took his hand. Gave it a second look. "How long this scratch infected?"

He glanced down at the swollen red streak. Tried to remember cutting it. "Last night, I guess. When we found Cochran's car."

"Ah." Her fin felt soft, like ice-cold velvet. "Nano retrievers, small invasive, no pain. Hand here."

He pulled away. He had the insane urge to grab his girls and run. Stupid. Whatever he was running from had caught him.

THIRTY-ONE

THAT NIGHT DAVID DREAMED OF HIS FATHER.

He was walking through an airport; he had a plane to catch. It had been raining, but the sun was out and he could see through the plate-glass window that the tarmac was rain-streaked, but drying.

He had just veered to the right when he saw his father, on the left side of the corridor, smiling quietly, waiting to be noticed.

"Dad?"

Someone tried to interrupt them but his father pointed a finger and they froze, silenced.

His father looked good. Trim, rested, healthy. David put his arms around him and hugged him, then pulled back and looked into his father's face.

"How can you be here if you're dead?"

His father's eyes were kind, he was smiling. "If you need me to be alive, David, I'm alive."

The phone rang, jerking David awake. The dream went like a bubble popping in his head. He reached for the receiver, aware of the sweat-drenched sheets, the oily moisture coating his skin, Rose in the bed by his side.

She had not slept near him in months. He would ponder this miracle later.

He took a deep breath. "Hello?"

"Detective Silver? Detective Silver?"

He tried to place the voice. An old man, upset, almost in tears. He thought for a confused moment of his dad.

"Is this Detective Silver? *Please* answer me, please, sir."

"Yeah, this is Silver." David sat up, rubbed his face. "It's okay, I'm here. Who is this?"

"It's Mr. Dandy. You gave us all your number, sir. You said we could call."

David heard an angry scream, the wail of a terrified child. He was instantly awake.

"What is it, Mr. Dandy? What's going on?"

"It's *you*. You people!"

"Please?"

"Valentine said to call. The police are here and they broke down the door. Please, Detective, don't let them take that child from Annie Trey."

"Broke down the door?" David said. Nobody went through doors anymore.

"They used a battering ram, sir." Dandy's voice broke. "For God's sake, can't you hear these babies cry?"

THIRTY-TWO

DAVID STAYED ON THE RADIO ALL THE WAY IN, CAR LIGHTS
blazing through the black void of four-thirty A.M., August
haze milky in the headlights.

Della's voice floated up from the console. "David? You
there?"

"Here."

"Where is 'here'? I'm not tracking right."

"Just outside Watson, moving past the Ritter projects to
Cracker Village."

"Don't be going in there by yourself. I'm sending uniforms."

"The hell you are. Not in that area—uniforms will start
a firefight for sure. You send an army or let me slip in by
myself."

"David, I talked to Vice—they got nothing running right
now, and they haven't used battering rams since 1997."

"Maybe the one you talked to doesn't know what's up."

"And maybe you're being set up."

"I heard babies crying, Della."

He left his car out front, wondered if it would be there when
he got back. It was hot out, muggy, and he was sweating
before he left the air-conditioned coolness of the car. He
put a hand on his gun, let it register his prints so it would
be ready to fire when he needed it.

The outside door of the tenement hung crookedly,
knocked off the hinge. The building was completely dark,
no power. David's heartbeat quickened, and he went cau-
tiously into the cavernous entrance foyer.

Broken glass underfoot announced his presence. He took
his flashlight out, made his way upstairs.

It was the quiet that alarmed him. No televisions, no

music, no voices raised, no cries of children, cranky, tired, or afraid. It was a tense quiet, as if the residents were holding their breath. He pictured them inside their hot, dark apartments, huddled together, afraid to open their doors. It was the kind of quiet he felt around a freshly murdered corpse—the air electric with recent emotion.

He took the stairs slowly, beam of light from his flash bobbing ahead, making him a target. He listened, thought he heard something, paused in the hallway.

Singing. He recognized Valentine's voice.

She was singing hymns, slow and sweet with a throaty resonance. He cupped his palm over the light, turning his fingers a glowing orange, pointed the flash at the floor, and crept quietly down the hallway.

They were huddled together in Valentine's apartment—Mr. Dandy, Annie, Eddie Eyebrows, and two tiny, sleepy little girls—Jenny and Cassidy, side by side next to Valentine, curled up on the floor. The door was open, as were the windows, creating a cross ventilation that almost made the room bearable.

Watching them from the hallway, David felt chill bumps along his arms. They'd lit a candle that gave off the faint scent of violets. They had that look about them, a sort of exhausted abandon one saw in victims of catastrophe.

Annie was curled in almost fetal position, arm across Jenny, who had her head on Annie's arm. Both were tucked close to Valentine, who was leaning against the back of a beige velvet couch that made you want to curl up and watch TV or read a book. Cassidy's head was in Valentine's lap, and Valentine stroked the child's neck and hairline with a languid touch that David thought must feel like heaven.

Mr. Dandy was sitting upright, sound asleep, facing the door. He held a large stick, slack in one hand. His shirt was torn, one suspender slipping. He had taken his shoes off and they sat, unlaced and worn, on either arm of the chair. Eddie Eyebrows had the couch, and lay sideways, one hand tucked under his cheek. Childish and odd-looking on a man his age, but suitable for the child inside.

Valentine looked up and saw David, standing in the hallway, shielding the light. Her face was mysterious and beautiful in the flickering candlelight. She quit singing—something slow about Jesus and angels keeping little children safe in the night—and hummed softly.

David had that awful after-the-fact feeling—common occurrence for a homicide cop, always called in when the worst was over.

He shined his light toward Annie Trey's apartment, and caught his breath.

The door was off the hinge, on the floor in pieces. David closed his eyes, wondering if there had been a shout or a knock, any kind of warning before the door had been smashed open. One part of his mind replayed Mr. Dandy's voice, frantic and frightened, the cries of the frightened little ones in the background. The other part wondered what they, whoever they were, had used as a battering ram.

David walked in carefully, shining his light around the apartment, getting a sketchy but horrific illumination of the raid. The rocking chair was over on its side, old green cushion torn, hanging off the side. The plastic couch had been overturned, jammed up into the corner, one leg bent—when it was turned right side up, it would list to the left in a permanent wobble. Children's toys were scattered, most of them broken, trampled by large careless feet.

"They wore dark blue flak jackets, with 'Police' stenciled in gold on the back."

He hadn't heard her behind him, and he jumped at the sound of Valentine's voice. She leaned against the doorjamb, close enough to touch. She was smoking a cigarette, the orange glow drawing his eye. The acrid smell of the smoke filled the hallway. There were no smokers' "friends" in the complex. She could light up without being doused by sticky grey foam, the usual lot of anyone who had the bad manners and worse sense to smoke in the modernized public areas, or multiple residentials.

He saw her hands moving in the darkness, bringing the cigarette to her lips, taking it away.

"Made a mess, didn't they?"

David flashed his light around the apartment. "Tell me what happened," he said, and she sighed.

THIRTY-THREE

THEY SAT ACROSS FROM EACH OTHER LIKE CONSPIRATORS, cross-legged, right under the painted-on window and the small hole that went through the wall. It was hot—David had seen sweat beading on Valentine's skin in a flash of the light, but he was shivery and cold.

"I was just home from work. Been inside to change my dress and shoes. Cassidy was asleep at Annie's place. I was on my way over to pick her up, when I heard a noise like a train coming through, and I heard Annie scream." She took a breath. "You know what I thought? I thought a plane had hit the building. I came outta my place expecting everybody to be dead. And it's funny, but the whole time it was going on, I kept thinking, oh happy girl, 'cause nobody is dead." She laughed, low and deep in her throat. "Cassidy was crying and carrying on, and the men are yelling they heads off, and I'm almost laughing, don't ask me why."

David could make out the barest outline of her face in the darkness. He looked out the small hole, saw the lights of the next building. Nothing else on the block was affected. Everyone else had power.

No accident that.

"They were yelling and stomping around."

"Elaki or human?"

"Men. Human. 'Bout six of them, big guns. Loud and scary. Told everybody to lay down on the floor. Saw me, told me the same. They stomped around like they were looking for something, but . . ."

David turned away from the window. "But what?"

He saw her shoulders move. A shrug?

"Just got a funny feeling, like they were going through the motions. Look in one cabinet, but not the other. The

135

closet, but not the shower stall. Didn't rip open the mattresses, but stomped all over the toys, even though I honestly think they were trying not to.

"Then the power shuts off. Annie's crying. Cassidy is crying. But Jen is quiet, which is worse, the more you want to think about it."

David nodded.

"And then they left."

David frowned. "Anything missing?"

Valentine made a rude noise. "How we going to tell? What we got to steal? The worse problem we got when the dust settles and we're sure the men are gone, is we can't find Jenny's bear."

THIRTY-FOUR

DAVID WENT HOME BUT DID NOT SLEEP. EVERY TIME HE drifted off, he would wake suddenly, coated in sweat, kick off the covers, turn the air conditioning up, then wake up ten minutes later so cold his teeth chattered. Worse than the sweats and the chills was the tight panic in his chest, the breathlessness.

And here, when he really needed the bed all to himself, and certainly had no desire for sex, Rose decided to stay with him. He knew he was impossible to sleep with, knew he was keeping her up. Twice he suggested, gently and with tact, that one of them take refuge on the couch. She'd pretended not to hear.

Instead she brought him blankets when he was cold, ice chips when he was hot, and once a cup of tea with honey and whisky.

He'd finally drifted off around dawn in a comfortable, peaceful sleep, waking at nine-thirty to a house that was quiet, and warming up with sunlight.

He had not heard Rose get up with the kids, had not heard their typically noisy preparations for school. Everyone had been quiet. Everyone had been considerate. He'd had a good sleep, and had awakened almost refreshed.

But by the time he walked into the office at eleven, the drive in had worn him down, and his heart was racing in his chest.

He stood in the elevator, wondering if he should turn around and go home.

With Miriam missing? No sign of Cochran? Men, disguised as police officers, battering down Annie Trey's door?

Yeah, right.

David looked around the bullpen, saw String headed out

the back way. "String? Where is everybody?"

The Elaki skidded on his bottom fringe, rotated like a bird, and looked at him. "Detective David arrives, most good. Is the round-up conferencing. Follow and I will show."

The room was full. Walker, String, Mel, Sam Caper, the forensic mechanic named Vanessa, Della, and David. They'd had to bring in extra chairs from one of the larger conference rooms. The meeting over there was smaller, but it was about identity theft, which was highly funded at the moment. All the rage (meaning anger—an in-cop joke) with the general public, which meant that's where the action would be for a while.

David closed his eyes, listening for the umpteenth time to the 911 emergency call Annie Trey had made the night Cochran disappeared. Her voice sounded sluggish and soft. David knew without looking again that the stress-level readout was off the charts. She'd been having a four Valium night.

Her voice cracked when she mentioned the three Elaki. David wondered how Thurmon had hardened his heart to her evident distress. Even with a heavy caseload, there should have been more follow-up.

Next on the agenda were Miriam's messages—except there weren't any. No record of the call Annie Trey swore she'd made. David looked at Mel.

"Somebody stopped her newspapers, Mel. Stopped her mail. Erased those messages, if there were any."

"There were. I left some of them."

String slid toward Mel. "Then who would be the stopper of the newspapers and mail?"

"I called and tried to check on that. Come to find out she has an automatic thing. If she don't pick up the mail and stuff for three days, they automatically stop. Why, you don't think I followed that up? You think I'm too stupid to live or something?"

"We're just kicking it around, Mel. Just trying to work it out."

"Yeah, sorry. So where is she?"

Della chewed a fingernail. "Hiding?"

"Makes sense," David said.

Mel blew air through his teeth. "Why hasn't she been in touch?"

"Maybe she's scared whoever killed Cochran would come after her. If it's a blood sanction—"

"They *had* her," Mel said. "They had both of them. That's the flaw in the logic, folks. The people she'd be in hiding from had her in their hands. If she was in danger from them, then what was going to happen happened. The simplest explanation is the one that's usually right."

"So where is the body?" David said.

"Side by side with Cochran in a ditch somewhere."

The way Mel said it was chilling.

"Let's show the hologram," Vanessa said.

Someone called "Lights out." The smell of strong coffee made David queasy, even as he sipped it from a mug. The outside door opened, throwing a band of light across the hologram.

Captain Halliday shut the door softly, pulled the only empty chair up close to David.

"Any luck?" David whispered.

Halliday shook his head. "If it was a legitimate police operation, nobody's admitting it. I've had feelers out since you called in last night. Bottom line is it sounds like cops, but nobody's owning up to it. I honestly think that if it was something under wraps, I'd have gotten a hint, maybe warned off. I think it was a scam, David, top to bottom. You say they didn't take anything?"

"Nothing to take," David said. "You seen this?" He inclined his head toward the hologram.

"No. But it's breaking my heart, if that was Miriam in the trunk. How's Mel holding up?"

"Hanging by his fingernails."

On-screen, a dark, shadowy figure was moving through a hole in the trunk, elbows catching, just as the shadow emerged into the back seat.

The car's interior burst into malevolent shadows moving

frantically. The action was hard to make out.

"Any chance this Annie Trey is into some kind of drug thing?" Halliday asked.

"Come on, Captain. If it was a drug burn, they'd have killed everybody in the apartment. And Annie Trey wouldn't be dirt poor. Della's been over her records of purchase for the last six months. That kid is hanging on by the skin of her teeth, no question."

"Cochran had money?"

"None recorded, but he had things. Expensive tennis shoes. The Visck, that car."

"Which—there it goes. Right over the guardrail."

A low-pitched moan rippled around the room, in sympathy for either the beautiful car or the occupants, David wasn't sure which.

Someone called up the lights.

"No real information there," Vanessa said. She had her hair tied back again today, and David thought of Miriam. She always wore her hair tied back.

"Nobody was killed by the crash, you've established that," Della said.

"Point," String said.

David wondered if the Elaki was keeping score or using a human expression. He noticed that everyone avoided looking at Mel.

Vanessa cleared her throat. "I do have some interesting information for you. One is, I've got a match on soil samples, taken off the car. We found dirt in the top of the wheel wells, and matched it to what was on the tools in the trunk. The best news is, I can tell you exactly *where* the soil came from."

Mel looked at her. "How the hell can you do that?"

She smiled. "I'd like to say I'm brilliant, but it's insecticides."

"Insecticides are banned," Halliday said.

"Exactly. Except in certain parks and preservation areas, and those sprayings are strictly scheduled. This area got hit no more than six weeks before the digging was done. We-'ve tracked it to the old Bailey Farmstead."

Mel sat forward. "You're sure, right? No doubt?"

String rolled sideways. "But this is not the sensical. Isss long way of distance from Elaki-Town. No any nearness to the university. So what could be the draw?"

Vanessa tugged her ponytail to one side. "What you have there is a preserved turn-of-the-century farm community, complete with farmhouses, outbuildings, crops, and orchards. Hence the insecticides. What it has to do with your players, I haven't the slightest. But there's no question where that soil came from."

David frowned. Something was ringing a bell, something at the edge of his awareness. There was a connection he ought to be making.

God, his head hurt. He rubbed his temples. Whatever it was, wasn't coming. Maybe he'd get it later.

"So you think Luke Cochran was digging there or something?"

"Maybe. We know he was there," Vanessa said. "There's a generous amount of Cochran's blood mixed in with the soil. And Elaki scales. The interesting thing is, Caper tried to get a scale match, from the soil sample and the three Elaki that took Cochran away in the car."

"And?" Halliday said, shifting sideways in his chair.

Vanessa shook her head. "No go. The Elaki involved in the digging wasn't one of the three who picked Cochran up. We know the car was out there at the farmstead, from the soil we found up in the wheel well, but it never showed in the car's black box. So I analyzed the navigational program, making sure the car had no record of being out there. And I found it. Layered in and covered up, but it was there. Which is interesting, that somebody tried to hide that."

"You sure about that?" David asked.

Della was nodding. "I looked at the program myself. Somebody tried to wipe it out of the memory. Somebody who knew Cochran's code."

"Cochran?" David asked.

Della shrugged. "Why?"

David frowned. "Can you tell when, exactly, the car was out there?

Della shook her head. "Nope. Could have happened at any point."

"How about in the middle of that scenario we just watched?" Mel's voice was thick.

"If you're asking me could the sequence be wrong, could the car have been to and from the Bailey Farmstead after they picked up Cochran, and before the car went over the guardrail, the answer is yes."

Mel took a hard breath. Looked at David.

"Don't jump to conclusions," David said. His throat was sore. He took another sip of coffee.

"Maybe those three Elaki took them out there and buried the bodies," Mel said.

David set his coffee cup down gently. "Take it easy, Mel. If they did that, why leave the car parked at the Elaki-Town exit? Why leave the tools in the trunk?"

Della was nodding her head. "David's right, Mel, it makes no—"

Walker slid to one side, close in to String. She said something in low tones David could not quite make out. Soften the blow?

String rose up on his bottom fringe. "Please to call attention. Is to make the sense if killing retaliation the blood sanction. Is to smack the face with the factuals. An oblique taking of credit. Saying we have done this. Beware us."

"Jesus," Mel said. "They buried them."

"Vanessa, were there any other blood traces?" David asked.

Mel blew air between his teeth. "You know, if you mean Miriam, say it. You find traces of Miriam's blood in those soil samples, Vanessa? Caper?"

"No."

"No."

"You look?"

"I looked," Caper said.

Halliday looked at David, which meant everyone else did too. He wiped sweat from his upper lip.

"What do you think, David?"

"Have Sifter Chuck brought in."

THIRTY-FIVE

DAVID WAS HEADED DOWN THE HALL TOWARD MEL WHEN Halliday tapped his shoulder.

"David, could you stop by my office just a minute?"

"Sir, I'm sorry about the pig incident. The thing was—"

"David. This isn't about the pig."

"Oh."

"Aslanti. She's helping unofficially, right?"

"Right."

"She's here. She wants to see you."

"Now? Here now?"

"Yeah. I offered to let her come into the conference room and give us her findings, but she . . . evidently she wants to see you privately. She was very insistent. So I put her into my office. Told her you'd be right up. David?"

"Yeah?"

"You went a little green there. You okay?"

"Just long hours, no sleep. I'm fine." David headed for the elevator, then veered toward the stairwell. He didn't want to look at anybody's face.

Someone, Aslanti he figured, had lowered all the blinds in Halliday's cubicle, making the square office small, dark, and claustrophobic. David closed the door reluctantly, surrendering to the dreariness.

Aslanti had wedged herself into a corner behind Halliday's chair.

David looked at her. "I get the feeling you have bad news."

She slid back and forth. "The human attempts humor?"

"Not so I noticed. Does this seem funny?"

"Silver the Detective David, please do not joke me. Have news that be the formidable." A stillness came over her.

David braced himself.

"In blood testing have found the evidence of you in disease."

It was odd, his overwhelming urge to grin at her, even to laugh. Part of his mind told him to get serious. He just didn't know how.

"What disease am I in?" he asked.

She turned her back on him in exquisite Elaki courtesy. "Is a bacteria/virus hybrid, common on Elaki home planet, all Elaki immunize against as pouchling embryo."

He took a deep breath. "There's a vaccine, then?"

She waved a fin in a thin, fluting motion that conveyed a distress that should have warned him.

"This is Elaki vaccine only. Isss not to be translatable to the human physiology."

David sat down on the couch. The lights were dim. He wondered if Aslanti had ordered them up that way, or if the system still needed work.

He looked at his hands. "Help me out here, Aslanti. I'm not sure what questions to ask."

"You want all knowledge, no pit-patting about?"

"No pit-patting," David said. "Tell me."

She was silent a moment. "Isss bad thing, most toxic, destructor of internal organs in most advanced form of virulence."

"Is it what killed Annie Trey's infant son?" His use of the term infant son snagged him. Cop distancing technique, he realized, something he did automatically. If he said "tiny little baby boy Hank," it would hurt him.

Aslanti was talking. "For sure, cannot say without my own tests to run. After the long look of the notes of Miriam, and some discreet talking to other medicals, my guess is most yes."

"Is this . . . is this definitely fatal, then?"

"Do not know, Detective David. The human will have none of the exposure, nothing like this in physical histories, so no antibodies or defenses built up." Her voice rose. "So you body have the complete defenselessness. So very vulnerable you are, most sorry."

David laced his fingers together. His mouth was dry.

"Last night. The other night you asked me about my pouchlings." God, they had him doing it. "About my *children*. How contagious is this?"

"Not very, and danger is minimal trace to female species human or Elaki."

David felt dizzy for a moment, just sitting still. "You're sure?"

"Of the absolute most."

He took a deep breath. Felt almost happy. Almost.

"Your Rosebud wife and three shiny pouchlings—childrens—are to be most safe. Female can be infected, but worst symptoms to be the respiratory irritation."

"Like a bad cold?"

"Yesss."

"Oh," David said. Little Jenny Trey had had a bad cold.

"Isss not to be easy, this transmission. If careful, family not go even to the cold stages. Can make you noninfectious."

"You can?"

"But yes. That at least is able."

"I want that."

"Small decline chances of survival. Not much, but is to be considered."

"I don't want to take any chance on giving this to anyone."

She was quiet. "Right decision, Detective David."

"So how did I get it?" He looked at her. "Look, you can turn back around, Aslanti. I'm okay. I'm not going to embarrass you."

"My wish is not to be causing you the embarrass."

"Tell me how I got this."

She still would not turn around. "Obvious be the Trey family. Transmission must go through you the blood, mix blood from infector, in some rare case saliva."

He looked at the deep scratch healing on the back of his hand.

"Big question, Detective, is how was infection absorbed by the baby Hank. You must understand how intensive be the screen before on-planet presence allowed. No unvaccinated Elaki allowed entrance permission.''

"Could it be transmitted on things, like a child's toy? A teddy bear?''

"Iss vague the possibility. For the short time periods, during weather hot conditions, as now. But not long times before bacteria/virus agent die down dead. Also, all possessions put through screening freeze, none are the exceptions. Have to be live organism of infection on here this planet. Of a scariness to contemplate.''

"Some unvaccinated Elaki got through.''

"Unlikely this, Detective Silver David. All pouchling embryo, all, vaccinated.''

David ran his hand through his hair. He could not seem to think.

"Other disease vector include germ warfare mechanism. Possibly unlikely but possibly it is. Other disease vector is animal, but no animal allowed between planet for just such this reason.''

David frowned, some memory tugging. "What kinds of animals?''

"Only Elaki animal creatures. The Bredit fur-bearing reptile, some insect, and of course, trillopy.''

"Trillopy?''

"Predator, dangerous this. Not tame. Not allowed, presence controlled even home, most careful.''

"But String said something about a trillopy the night we found Cochran's car. He heard some kind of noise, a whistle or a trill, some kind of cooing whine. He thought it sounded like a trillopy.''

At last she turned to look at him, belly rigid. "You are to be sure?''

"String wasn't sure, he didn't see it.''

"Coincidence too big.'' One eye prong twitched. "If so, the trillopy here, is most bad and upper high hand dangerous.''

"Because of the disease?''

"Dangerous animal. Like lion loose in place of nursery pouchlings.''

"If one was running loose, we'd hear reports of some kind."

"Yesss. So if here, is in control. Some are kept as—petters, you call it?"

"Pets."

"Pets. By the rich eccentric loony tunes."

David looked at her. "I take it there's no treatment?"

"Take it wrongly."

He tried to keep his voice calm. "I thought you said there's no vaccine for humans."

"Isss other broadside treatment."

David chewed his bottom lip. Reminded himself that human doctors were no better—too much medical jargon and too little time for explanations. If you could get in to see one.

"We have too many varieties to have medicines or vaccines specific. Develop combat for one, ten more to show their tails, eh? So the broadside treatment is the freeze-dry."

"Like they do food packages?"

"Some difference apply to living tissues wishing to keep alive."

"Yeah," David said hoarsely.

"Iss process selective. Goes for the invading hybrid, attention specific. Body wastes out the freeze-dry offenders. Problem be this—maybe not all be targeted and got. Not good for body the continuous treatment. So if enough freezed away, then body takes care of ones left. Boost immunities with drug treatments. But if not enough killed gone, or body weak, then overwhelm the immune, attack organs internal, and deteriorate to death."

David cleared his throat. "But there's a chance."

"Yesss."

He thought for a moment. "Just what are my odds, Aslanti?"

She began to sway from side to side. "Do not find such a calculating prediction at all possible, Detective Silver David. I be most alarmed for you yessss, but I be ready to fight for you, yesss. The best to do now is let disease have way to the body and reach a certain peak momentum. At this point the new chemical messages in disease communication make change from procreate to survive. This crucial the point be. Change from procreate then freeze before virulence takes the hold. If miss some not so able to make lots new, because now in survival mode. If body can focus, maybe win.''

"So what you're saying is, I wait until I get worse, then I go through the freeze-drying thing, and I survive it or I don't.''

"Not quite the dry cut. Can win out total. Can have the chronic constant up and down. Or can be fine, then time elapse and hidden ones flourish and flare.''

He was having trouble catching his breath.

"Am sorry to be, Detective Silver David. You say no pit-pat.''

"How hard is it to make me completely noncontagious? I mean, is it complicated, does it take—''

"Have brought with me proper air injection, will have the effect of immediacy.''

"Thank you for that," David said, and meant it.

THIRTY-SIX

DAVID'S FIRST IMPULSE WAS TO GO HOME AND HUG HIS little girls. He had been impatient while Aslanti fumbled over the injection. Time was wasting. He might not have all that much.

He thought, on the way home, as the scenery went by much too slowly, of obscure, remote tribes of people wiped out by marauding anthropologists, even into the 1980's, with measles the typical culprit. AIDS, before the vaccine. Cancer. The plague.

He thought of Annie Trey, losing her child and vilified as a baby killer. He was getting angry. His grip on the steering wheel was tight enough that his hands ached.

He wanted Teddy, and now it was too late. Calling her now would be emotional blackmail, unforgivable. *Love me, please, I may be dying.* Why hadn't he called her before, just to say hello, so what's the big deal?

He wondered how the disease would progress. Would it attack his brain? Would he get moody and unpredictable, like his mother? Would he be unkind to his children? What would it do to them, watching their father die?

Rose knew, as soon as he came into the kitchen, that something was very wrong. He was not surprised. They had been married a long time.

The kids weren't home—they were in school; he'd managed to forget that. His only thought had been to see them, and they weren't there. He considered taking them out of school. Too upsetting for them, he decided. Disruptive.

Rose was watching him. "You want to talk in here?"

"Fine."

They sat across from each other at the kitchen table. It had not been wiped after breakfast, and there were sticky rings of milk, and a smear of grease.

"I'm sick, Rose."

"Sick?" She nodded. "I thought you were coming down with something last night."

She didn't get it.

"I mean that I have a serious and possibly fatal something or other—it's a sort of virus/bacterial hybrid. The girls are safe, so are you. It's only fatal to males."

She went rigid. "*Fatal.*"

"I'm a long way from dead, Rose." He touched his chest, smiled at her. "Heart still beating. I've got a good chance of pulling through this."

"But, where did—"

"It's a long story. Would you like a cup of coffee?"

She nodded slowly. "And talk fast, will you?"

He knew what she meant. She wanted every question answered all at once. He'd felt the same way in Halliday's office.

It calmed him, the physical and familiar act of making coffee. Focusing on Rose made it easier not to worry about himself. He had a lot of ground to cover. The days when he'd confided every detail of his work were long gone.

For a while, just a short while, it was like the old days between them, except that while he talked she cried very unobtrusively, tears streaming down her cheeks. She was quick, she understood police work. They could talk in a sort of professional shorthand, and when he told her something, she knew exactly what he meant. He had missed these conversations.

Eventually the talk wound down. David's throat was sore. There was a long silence between them.

"How do you feel now?" she asked.

He shrugged. "I don't know."

"Maybe you should rest. You didn't get much sleep last night."

He stared at the floor. Sleep was not attractive. Sleep was not what he wanted to do with the rest of his life. He took a sip of coffee. He'd made it strong and it was cold now, tasted horrible.

"Look, David. I know things aren't great between us. I

just . . . you know I'll take care of you. I'll get you through this.''

"You don't have to be nice to me, Rose."

"I'm not being *nice*, David."

"Feel sorry for me? Every night I come home, you *throw* something at me. And *now* you're going to take care of me?''

"Get real, David. *Yes*. I feel sorry for you. Tell me you have a potentially fatal illness, tell me you might die—I'm not going to feel *sorry*?'' Her eyes were red-rimmed, bathed in tears. "You're posturing, David. You're angry, so you're going to project it all on me. I don't accept it and I don't deserve it."

"Now who's posturing?"

He left her sitting at the kitchen table, slammed the door on his way out. He never slammed doors; he'd had that tendency drummed out of him in childhood, and he didn't tolerate it in his kids. But Rose did it all the time. He'd expected to enjoy it more.

He went to a far, dark corner of the barn, burrowed in the corner, pulled the filthy bedspread off his old Triumph. The motorcycle didn't run anymore, it needed work. As he recalled, it hadn't needed all that much; he just hadn't been able to get to it.

He blew dust off the seat. No time like the present.

THIRTY-SEVEN

DAVID WAS UP TO HIS ELBOWS IN GREASE WHEN HIS CHEST got tight and his breath started coming short and fast. He felt heat spread through his body, wondered if his face was as red as it felt. He put his wrench down, sat on a moldy bale of hay that had been in the barn since they'd bought the property. His hands were shaking.

He had actually forgotten, just for a little while, but the shadow was back. He was sick, and his children were going to watch him die.

He checked his watch, was astounded to see that the children had been home from school a while now. He was suddenly reluctant to see them.

He imagined the days ahead. How he would feel. How the kids would feel, watching. There would be times where they'd all be convinced he would beat this. And down times, where they'd all be afraid of his death.

Was it kind to drag them down with him? Easier for everyone, himself included, if he went off on his own a while, till he won or till he lost.

He was in the bedroom packing when he heard or felt a presence. Lisa stood in the doorway, barefooted, book tucked under one arm. Her hair was braided, coming loose. Her shirttail was out. She noted the open suitcase on the bed and looked up at him, and he thought he would re-member the look on her face for the rest of his life.

"I knew this was going to happen. You're leaving us, aren't you, Daddy?"

He sat down on the edge of the bed, clutching the sides of the mattress. He held out his arms and she came to him, hugged him tight.

"I'm not going to let you go, Daddy."

"I'm sick," he said softly. He patted the edge of the bed

and she sat down beside him. He saw ink on her hands, where she'd written herself a note to get her math test signed. "Mama and I were going to talk to you guys all together. But I have a very bad sickness. It's something you can't get, so you don't have to worry."

"I wouldn't care, Daddy. Please don't go."

"This sickness is very bad, Lisa. Sometimes when people get it they die. I'm just going for a while, till I get better."

"Are you going to the hospital?"

"Not yet, maybe later."

She pushed her glasses up on her nose. "Then where are you going?"

"I just need to get away for a while. Be by myself."

"Is this divorce stuff?"

Cut to the bottom line, every time. David smiled weakly. "I'm going to get sicker, I think, before I get better. I don't want you to have to see that."

"I think you're mad at us."

He grabbed her shoulders. "At you kids? Of course not. Not at *all*. How could you think that?"

"But don't you love us? Us kids?"

"Yes, of course—you know I do."

"Then why are you leaving, Daddy? What if you do die? Don't you want to be with us some first?"

He was going to tell her that it wasn't about her, or about Mattie or Kendra or even Rose. He was going to give her a garbage speech about a man facing up to mortality, when he realized that he was kidding them all. It was about them, it was exactly about his difficult wife and his precious children. He didn't want to see their pain when he had enough of his own.

He looked at Lisa. Crossed his legs and leaned back. "The truth is, kidlet, I'm scared."

"Of dying?"

"I'm scared of my children watching me die."

She nodded; it made perfect sense to her, but she wasn't through with him yet.

"You can't go."

''No?''

She shook her head. ''You love us, right?''

''Yeah.''

''You want to be with us?''

He hesitated. Nodded.

''Then that's that.'' She went to his bag, and began to unpack.

THIRTY-EIGHT

THEY HAD A FAMILY DINNER, A RARE EVENT THESE DAYS in the Silver household. David did not eat much, Rose even less. But the children, being children, forgot the shadow, ate like field hands, and laughed a lot. Rose had given everyone the same meal tonight—pot roast, mashed potatoes. Comfort food. They were going to have pie and ice cream for dessert.

David and Rose finished with coffee on the back porch.

"How do you think the kids are taking it?" Rose said.

David shrugged. "Too early to tell. But they volunteered to do the dishes and they're all getting along."

Rose took a sip of coffee. "Yeah. They're taking it hard."

"They don't really believe it," David said.

"Me either."

Dead Meat groaned and David scratched the dog's neck. "He really is a pretty good dog, even if he did eat my garden." The tightness in his chest came suddenly. He took a deep, hard breath.

"David? You okay?"

"It'll pass, just need a minute."

She watched him. "What does it feel like?"

"I'm hot, then I'm cold. Then hot and cold all at once, which is weird. Doesn't seem physically possible. Then I sweat, and then I shake and my teeth chatter. My chest feels tight, kind of frantic, like some kind of panic attack. Sometimes I ache. That enough symptoms for now?"

"David, what you said earlier. I want to get along with you. What if you do die? I want to be at peace with you, one way or another. It doesn't matter why, or what brings us to peace, just so we get there."

David put a hand on her leg. Nodded.

The sun was going down, the heat of the day turning loose. Yesterday he wouldn't have noticed. Today, he noticed too much. In all honesty, he liked yesterday better; he preferred taking things for granted. Before he'd had purpose, work to do, a case to solve. Now he had mortality. Big deal.

"Is there anything special you want, David?"

He looked at her. "What do you mean by that, Rose?"

"We could pull the kids out of school and go on a trip. Borrow money and do something crazy."

"And leave you guys in debt? I don't think so."

"If it makes you happy, I don't care. Tell me what you want, and let's do it. I'm serious."

She was leaning close, and he thought suddenly how sweet she could be. She had stayed up with him all night the night before. He had not heard word one about contagion fears, worries about what she would do on her own, how she would work if she was looking after him.

"What are you thinking, David?"

He looked at her and they both laughed. " 'What are you thinking?' My favorite marital question, second only to 'Do you think I should get my hair cut?' but nowhere near as dangerous as that all-time favorite, 'Do these jeans make me look fat?' "

She gave him a hard shove. "Come on, David, get serious."

"I've had enough serious for one day, thank you very much."

"No, but David. If there's something you want."

"I want my life back, Rose. I want to find Miriam, and Luke Cochran, and work like a maniac, and come home to you and the girls." I want Teddy, he thought, but didn't say it.

"So do it." She waved her hands in the air. "Wish granted."

He looked at her.

"I mean it. As long as you want it that way, as long as you can stay on your feet. You can't be easy with Miriam missing, I know you. You haven't lost your life, David, unless you give it up.''

"You don't care?"

"Of course I *care*. I don't mind. I mean, we could all sit in the kitchen and stare at each other. But.''

"And I want to work on my motorcycle. Do things with my hands.''

"Have at it.''

"I'm going to take some money out of savings, just a little, not much. I want to buy things, little things, for you and the girls.''

"Not me. Buy stuff for the kids, spend the money on them.''

"On whatever I want, which means you too. Okay?''

"Okay.''

"And I want homemade mashed potatoes every night.''

"Don't push your luck.''

He laughed. "Just testing.''

THIRTY-NINE

DAVID KNEW, WHEN HE WALKED INTO THE BULLPEN, THAT
Aslanti had told. It was there in Della's eyes when he
walked toward his desk. It was there in the way String slid
toward him, then faltered. And while everyone else went
about their business, the three of them looked at each other
in silence.

"Hi, guys," David said finally.

Della moved toward him, eyes hard, chin up. She gave
him a quick, hard hug and he patted her back.

"*You* will get well. Is that clearly understood? You are
going to eat a lot of chocolate, and that's going to increase
the endorphins in your brain, to the point where your body
has to get better."

"Della Detective, you cannot—"

She looked at String. He slid backward, then reared up
on his bottom fringe.

"Yesss, most correct is the chocolate. Much of it."

" 'Bout time you showed up."

David turned, saw Mel trying to look at his watch and
not spill the two extra-large cups of coffee he was carrying.
He handed one cup to David, and smiled.

"We got work piling up, David," he said, tone brash
and friendly. "You picked a helluva morning to be late.
That Sifter Chuck guy's waiting in Three."

Was he was going to ignore it? David wondered. He gave
his partner a sidelong glance.

Mel took a large swallow of coffee. "We all got tested
yesterday afternoon, by the way. Should know by late today
if any of the rest of us are infected."

David felt a welcome sense of camaraderie, as if his illness was a mutual problem they all had to tackle.

Mel was still talking. "Nobody had any cuts or wounds,

like you did, and nobody else is having any symptoms, so Aslanti don't think there's much chance any of the rest of us got it.''

David nodded matter-of-factly, marveling that he actually felt matter-of-fact. ''I took that injection yesterday. So I'm not contagious.''

''Good thing,'' Mel said.

Della glared at him. ''As if we'd worry about that.''

Mel gave her a sour look. ''Get real, Della. This is a fatal disease.''

''Not always,'' she said quickly, looking at David.

Mel leaned forward in his chair. Motioned for them all to come close. He seemed so clearly confident, so in control—in contrast to his recent mental state—that they all drew toward him, to hear his low-pitched advice.

''Sentimental crap isn't going to help, is it, David?''

It was a rhetorical question, but David nodded anyway. Maybe a *little* sentimental crap would have been nice, but he liked the way Mel was setting the tone. It was comforting to find himself still in the everyday world, relationships the same as ever. He didn't really want everyone to be kind and tiptoe around him. He didn't want Della's chocolate.

Mel scratched his nose. ''Had a long talk with the captain yesterday. Sooner or later this virus thing is going to blow sky-high. He's already letting the Feds in on it, going through channels, whatever.''

''Be nice if he could wait till we get this case solved,'' Della said.

''Cannot let the raging of infection take hold,'' String said.

''The fact is,'' Mel said, ''and I got this from Halliday— the fact is, they're more than likely to be slow on this. Nobody's going to want to step on any Elaki toes—fringes, whatever. We'll probably have a free hand, we get on this. David, we all know you're sick. You work when you want, we carry you when you can't. We know you had that shot. I got no problem working with you one way or the other, and I just want to say that right out. You, Della?''

''Hey, I'm female, in case you forgot. It's nothing to me,

but for the record.'' She put her hands on her hips. ''I ought to smack you for even having to ask.''

''Have been Elaki vaccinized, but ditto the Della,'' String said.

Mel looked at David. ''You want to work this Sifter over, you and me?''

FORTY

MEL STOPPED ON THEIR WAY DOWN THE CORRIDOR. "HOW are you really?"

David shrugged. "Hell, I don't know."

"Rose and the girls?"

"Stiff upper lip. Kids don't really get it. How are you doing?"

"Thinking about Miriam night and day. Hoping I don't have to go to *her* autopsy."

"Maybe later we'll go get a beer."

Mel paused. "You know, I haven't had a drink since I read that list Miriam made. You remember, when she brought out all my bad points?"

"Sure. Forget I asked."

"Nah, hell, we got to do something when the world turns to utter crap. What do women do, when they're upset?"

"Eat. Eat chocolate."

Mel looked at David. "We could at least try it."

David followed Mel into Interview Room 3. Sifter Chuck was in a corner of the room, and David caught the side-angle view before the Elaki turned and faced them.

He knew he was a long way from being able to read Elaki as well as he read people, and yet. He still liked Sifter Chuck, even felt sorry for him. The Elaki was nervous, that frozen stillness had settled over him, but he turned toward them affably enough, waving a fin in the comradely Elaki Hi-sign.

"Much the greets, Detectives."

"Yeah, right." Mel headed for the Miranda-Pro, which hung over the edge of the table. He scooted it backward.

"How you doing?" David said. He gave Mel a wary look. He'd seen that intense attitude before.

David was tired, but feeling better than he had been. Aslanti had given him something to boost his immune system. Maybe it was helping. Maybe he was getting better. Maybe he wasn't as sick as everyone seemed to think.

"I have been done the rights advisement."

Mel nodded, checked the machine. Sat on the edge of the table. He spoke very softly.

"Mr. Sifter. Sir. I wonder if you have any objection to donating a scale or two for analysis by our crime-scene people?"

"I had been to think that here I was questions solely."

"Should I take that as no?"

David willed Sifter to agree. They could get scales from him through channels. It would look better for him if he agreed.

"I do not wish to submit with no explanations."

David felt his stomach drop. He still didn't believe Sifter Chuck had killed anyone.

Mel swung one leg. "You think we owe you an explanation? Let me ask you a question, then. What were you and Luke Cochran doing out at the Bailey Farmstead Preservation the day he disappeared?"

"Was not there."

David shook his head slowly. The Elaki twitched an eye prong, looked from David to Mel and back to Mel.

"You don't want to change your mind about that answer, do you?"

"Was not there."

"Was Cochran still alive then, or did you haul his body there yourself?"

"Isss dead? The Cochran isss dead?"

"We got a witness, saw you out there. We got a statement from Cochran's car, putting the two of you there."

One false, one half-true, David thought. Business as usual.

"We got soil samples and digging tools, and blood we've identified as Cochran's. We got Elaki scale samples I got no doubt are going to match with yours. So hold out if you want, but you can't change your DNA, my friend.

Soon as we get the match, you're going to be charged. You got nothing to say, that's fine.'' Mel looked at David. "I'll get the ball rolling. You coming?''

"Give me a minute.''

Mel nodded. Left without a backward look.

Sifter Chuck was swaying slightly, as if buffeted by an invisible wind. "Big macho tough guy, that one. *You got nothing to say, that's fine. I'll get the ball rolling.*''

David had never heard an Elaki imitate a human before. Sifter was good, very good. David tried not to smile, couldn't help himself. Bad cop, he thought. Bad policeman.

"How long have you been waiting here anyway?'' David asked him. "You hungry, want something to eat? Taco?''

"Elaki want a taco? Polly want a cracker? Have never seen with law trouble, Detective. Have been truthful all out with you on the statement. Do not understand why the treatment. Isss good cop bad cop this?''

David leaned back in his chair. "My partner has a personal relationship with the woman who's missing. He's upset. He thinks you're it. I don't think there's any way we're going to talk him out of that, unless you've got something you haven't given me?''

"Isss maybe time to up the shut.''

"That's your best bet. Unless . . . Never mind.''

"Unless?''

"It's not difficult, Sifter. If you killed Cochran, you ought to keep quiet, don't talk to us. Make us work for that scale sample, come up with our own motive, the whole drill. But here's what worries me.'' David got out of the chair, sat on the edge of the table, and leaned in toward the Elaki. "I've worked homicide a long time. Talked to a lot of people, been lied to regularly, stonewalled—and I'm not saying that's what's going on here, I'm just giving you a little friendly advice, Sifter. Most people we talk to have things they'd rather not discuss with the police. Everybody has secrets. The problem comes when these secrets make them withhold things we need to know. Even if you were innocent of anything else, withholding is obstruction of justice. And whatever it is somebody might be hiding, it might be something we'd be willing to overlook—if somebody deals with us on the up and up. But if not, if we don't get the real story without a lot of time and red-tape rigamarole, we come down hard.''

Sifter slid from one side of the room to the other.

David gave him a moment, then started up again. ''If there is a scale match, you're going to look pretty bad. I already explained, didn't I, that my partner has a personal interest here? That's going to make things pretty intense. We got tools out of Cochran's trunk. We've got blood, we've got soil samples. And we've got Luke's employer and supposed protector—that's you—who admits being with him the night he disappeared. I'll tell you the truth. We've gotten a lot of media attention on this thing. We're under pressure from our captain to wrap this up. And what we have, the best thing we have, Sifter Chuck, is you.''

The Elaki's inner belly quivered, then went rigid. David kept his voice gentle.

''Tell me.''

Sifter reared up on his bottom fringe, teetered for a moment, then let himself down slowly.

''Isss as you say. Some things would prefer to leave under the hide.''

''This is a murder investigation, Sifter. The only thing I'm interested in is Cochran's killer, because I know, the way a cop knows, my friend, I know this kid is dead.'' And as he said it, David realized it was true. ''I'm interested in one thing only. Finding his killer. Anything else comes up, I could not care less. You understand me?''

''Understand thisss, Detective. I do not have the knowledge of the Cochran eternal fate.''

''Did you go to the Bailey Farmstead with him the day he went missing?''

''Yesss. In afternoon.''

David waited.

''He left this place most alive.''

''What were you doing out there?''

Sifter did not answer.

''Look, Sifter, I need an explanation. We have soil, we

have blood. I can only think of one reason for those two substances. In my mind, I see Cochran dead and buried."

"Cochran will do the burying."

David looked at him, not quite sure what the Elaki was confessing to. "Go on."

"He and me together we did, with his work more of the tough physical."

"What about the blood?"

"Him be cut."

"Come on, Sifter, that's flimsy and you know it."

"Isss truth, flimsy or no. He feel not well, and get careless. Hand me shovel tool, cut him palm, all way cross. Bleed on tools, and into dirt tops. Keep dig, keeps bleed, and sweat in this head."

Sweat in this head? David kept going. "Why were you digging?"

"Make the deep hole."

David waited.

"Burying object."

"What object?"

"Bear."

"*What*?"

"Teddy bear."

FORTY-ONE

IT WAS NIGHTFALL BY THE TIME THEY GOT THEIR PERMIS-
sions, subpoenas, and crime-scene crew in place. It was
raining again.

Mel looked at David. "I don't believe for one minute
we're going to find any damn stuffed bears down there."

David coughed, huddled under the umbrella. "It's a
sleeper scam, Mel. I talked to the guys in Art Theft; they
said it's older than the antiques."

"They bury the loot, then discover it later?"

"That gives it authenticity. It's a twentieth-century farmstead, these are twentieth-century bears."

"Who'd believe somebody buried a damn teddy bear?"

"People who want to believe it. Dealers, Elaki dealers.
We're talking about a lot of money, Mel."

"Yeah, right."

The ground was soggy, and Sam Caper and his people
moved slowly in the soupy mud, preserving the dirt in layers, in case they found the worst.

David slogged through the grass onto an asphalt walk-
way and looked around. It was pretty here, providing you
could tune out the police cars, the CSU van, men and
women removing layers of mud, waiting for something
nasty to turn up. Mel was in the car, talking on the radio.
Keeping in touch with Halliday most likely. Sifter Chuck
had come over in the CSU van with String and Sam Caper.
The two Elaki were deep in conversation. Sifter Chuck had
that loose-limbed slump that signaled Elaki depression.

David walked through a puddle, wetting his feet. It was
too much like the night they'd found Cochran's car, the
night he'd become infected. No more than three or four
days ago. It seemed longer.

Sifter Chuck and Luke Cochran had done their digging

between the weathered grey barn and the bright yellow farmhouse—both under preservation and open to the public weekdays from ten to four-thirty. On weekends, the hours were extended till dusk.

It was peaceful out here, or would be, and well-tended, like David wished his place was. He liked the orderliness, though he knew it was dearly bought by government funds, and that the farm had looked nothing like this in the twentieth century, when it was a working operation.

There was a vegetable garden that made him think with a pang of the tender green plants in his own would-be garden, chewed to pieces by Dead Meat, the pretty good dog. Behind the house were the orchards, apples trees mainly. The path led that way. On his left was a small wooded area—trees fat, tall, and mature. David veered off the path, heading for the trees.

The rain stepped up just as he ducked under the tree cover. He could hear the roar of the raindrops as they launched a major onslaught, mercifully screened by the foliage. A steady drum of water thudded into his heavy black umbrella, but he was not deluged.

His feet were already soaked—not a great idea for a man as sick as he was supposed to be—but he couldn't get any wetter than he already was, and he wanted to walk.

It was like being in another world. The beat of the rain and the spread of trees shut out the noise of the city, and the CSU generators. It was dark, here in the trees, and David had not walked far down the rain-sloppy path when he had to call it quits. He leaned up against a tree and closed his eyes.

He felt hot and he couldn't quite seem to catch his breath. The hair at the back of his head was drenched with sweat and rain mist. He took his jacket off, breathing in the damp air, feeling chilly now. Sweat pooled under his arms and made the cotton shirt stick to his back. Hot and cold—he wished his system would settle on one or the other, and quit the continual switching that made it impossible for him to be comfortable.

The virus had not seemed real until now. He hadn't gone

more than two hundred yards, and his heart was pounding, his head aching. He was strongly considering sitting down at the base of this tree in the sticky mud for the pure joy of being off his feet.

He was a good hiker, a tireless hiker. He could tramp back and forth across his farm and think nothing of it. When he was well.

The rain had a smell to it, which for some reason made him think of the color grey. The raindrops kicked up little puffs of mud, and the earthy smell was strong, and not unpleasant.

David shivered, put his jacket back on, and zipped it up to the neck. He folded his arms. His teeth were chattering. His vision blurred and he rubbed his eyes, thinking how hot the skin of his palms felt on the clammy coolness of his forehead.

He took deep, steady breaths and began to feel a little bit better.

He liked it here, it was serene. He would like to be buried in a place like this.

David frowned. Something. Something was bothering him, something he ought to remember, but couldn't because he was so damn tired. He started shivering hard, and his muscles ached with the effort.

Someone was calling his name. He felt a hand on his shoulder.

"David?"

He tried to focus, rubbed his eyes. "Mel?"

"You okay?"

David licked his lips. "Yeah, sure."

"You're soaked, my friend. We better get you in out of—"

"What'd they find?"

Mel grinned. Held up a teddy bear lovingly wrapped in cellophane. "Sifter Chuck wasn't jerking us off after all. Broke his little Elaki heart to see this little fella dug up so soon. Cute, ain't it?"

David heard the relief in Mel's voice. No bodies. Miriam might still be alive.

"They got that bear wrapped too tight," David said. "Can't breath through plastic."

"That makes a lot of sense. Come on, let's get you out of here."

"Gotta rest a second."

"Throw your arm over my shoulder, buddy, there you go. Car's pretty close, once we get out of Bernheim Forest here. No, no, this way. Should have left a trail of bread crumbs, David, so you could find your way back. You're lucky I come along."

FORTY-TWO

DAVID SLEPT HARD ALL THE WAY TO MEL'S APARTMENT, a deep, heavy slumber that was like being drugged. He could feel the armrest of the car digging into his ribs, but could not wake up enough to shift position.

It was an effort to stand and wait while Mel talked to his locks. The door opened finally, and David did a double take.

"Am I still dreaming, Mel, or is your apartment clean?"

Mel grinned. "Walk through."

David looked at him over one shoulder, then went through. The neatness shimmered and was gone. An illusion. Here was the apartment David recognized—dirty laundry on the couch, vids stacked on every available surface, sticky kitchen floor. He knew that if he opened the refrigerator door, the kitchen would be flooded with bad smells.

"Home sweet home," Mel said, telling the door to lock.

"What happened there?" David said.

"Neatness hologram. Miriam gave it to me. Cute, huh? Somebody comes to the door, it looks like you got a nice place."

"Till you invite them in."

"Yeah, well, you want to get picky . . ." Mel pointed a finger. "Go get a hot shower. I'll leave some dry clothes for you, give Rose a call and tell her you're sleeping here tonight."

David headed into the bathroom. He was cold again. He turned the water on, undressed, and leaned against the wall of tiny dark blue tiles while hot water turned his skin pink and warmed him. When he was finished, he found that Mel had put a worn but clean pair of jeans on the toilet seat, along with an oversized white cotton shirt and a pair of white gym socks. The jeans were loose around the waist, and a little short in the leg. There was a small hole in the seat. But it felt good to be clean and in dry, comfortable clothes.

The hallway felt cool after the steamy heat of the bathroom. David rubbed his hair with what he hoped was a clean towel, felt the growth of beard on his face.

"You hungry?" Mel's voice floated in from the kitchen.

David yawned. His muscles felt loose, relaxed.

Mel stuck his head around the doorway. "Hey, I'm talking to you. Hungry?"

"Depends on what you got."

"Want some chocolate?"

David went into the kitchen. His face was still a healthy pink from the hot shower. "Did you say chocolate?"

"Yeah, remember? We decided to drown our sorrows like women do."

"*You* decided—"

"Go on, sit down inside. Just shove that laundry off the couch."

"Is it clean?"

"The couch?"

"Never mind."

"Oh, the laundry? Hell, I can't remember. Go on, I'll be right there."

David put the laundry in a chair on top of a stack of newspapers. He ordered the television to channel surf and settled on the couch. Mel dropped a chocolate bar in his lap, then sat on the other end of the couch, facing the TV.

"Channel surfing is no fun without a remote," David said.

Mel unwrapped his chocolate bar. "Come on, David, give this a chance."

David felt queasy. He broke his candy into small squares and pretended to eat. He looked at Mel.

"Well?"

"Well what?"

"How's it working? How do you feel?"

"Full."

They were quiet a while. Watched the weather on TV. It was hot and muggy in Kentucky, and the ragweed was bad.

"Maybe you have to eat more than one," Mel said finally.

"You can have mine."

"The hell. I got beer and Doritos in the kitchen.

Mel had offered the bed, but David opted for the couch. He had fallen right asleep. Less than an hour later he was suddenly wide awake, drenched in sweat, panicky and unsure of where he was. He walked around the dark apartment, ran a hand through his hair. Listened to Mel snoring in the next room.

Time was slipping by him, and he still didn't know where Miriam was, or if Cochran was dead or alive, and he was getting sicker by the hour.

He left Mel a note and summoned his car.

FORTY-THREE

VALENTINE SANG IN A CLUB CALLED THE DIXIE-SAIGON—
the kind of place you'd find nowhere else in the world but
Cracker Village. There were very few cars out front, the
locals didn't own cars. The place was packed to the legal
limit and beyond, and this on a week night.

Years ago in the deep South they'd have called the
Dixie-Saigon a juke joint. The tables were unmatched, the
floor uneven linoleum, but almost every chair was taken.
The walls had been painted, papered, and painted again,
giving them a texture that almost seemed planned.

David smelled stale beer and garlic, not a bad combination. He was still wearing Mel's tattered blue jeans, like
ill-fitting hand-me-downs, and he had a heavy growth of
beard. His eyes had been bloodshot and dark with fatigue
in the bathroom mirror at Mel's. He would blend in here.

It was hot inside the club. The windows that lined the
top of the wall were all open, and the smell of ozone and
hot, damp air poured in. A breeze started up, and David
found an empty chair. He could only feel the small draft
of air when he closed his eyes. It was faint enough that it
might have been wishful thinking.

There was a stage at the end of the room—a small one,
dark hardwood that had been polished so diligently it reflected the light. A skinny Asian man burst through the
swinging doors that led into the kitchen, and took the steps
up to the stage in one energetic leap. He wiped his hands
on a dirty apron. Sweat dripped from his pockmarked forehead.

"It is my deep pleasure to introduce to you our very
own, very talented, silver-tongued beauty . . . Miss *Valentine*."

The applause was amazing, considering how drunk the

patrons were. David was surprised they could find their
hands, much less coordinate movements. People whistled,
shouted happily. David watched the stage, wondering what
kind of act Valentine had.

It was not what he expected.

She wore a simple black dress that reached her calves.
It looked like silk and was slit up the right side. Her black
spike heels made her look slim and sexy. Standing in front
of an old-fashioned microphone in a round orb of spotlight,
she began to sing.

Opera.

Little Cassidy had said her mother sang in Italian, but
David hadn't made the connection. He listened, mouth
open.

He had always assumed he hated opera, but he had never
heard it sung like this. He was an instant convert.

The sound system was quite good—an astonishing feat
in a place like this. Valentine's voice rose and fell with a
clear, pristine purity. No one talked. No one even whispered. Everyone watched and listened, spellbound.

David wondered why she was singing in a place like the
Dixie-Saigon. She could sing anywhere in the world with
a voice like that. He looked at faces in the crowd, and knew
that for whatever reason she chose to sing here, she was
recognized as the miracle that she was.

David closed his eyes, let the room go away. He had
another moment, pure happiness; he'd thought his illness
would keep them from coming. He felt lucky to be here,
to be listening, to have found a chair near the window
where he could feel the breeze.

He opened his eyes so he could watch her. Her arms
were raised, eyes closed. He could not tell where the black
dress stopped and the shadows began. Her choice of cloth-
ing, lighting, were perfect. The voice was the focus, the
voice was all.

When she stopped singing, the room stayed silent; then
the applause began. Valentine turned and left the stage, as
if she could not hear the accolades, or simply did not care.

David felt wrenched when she left, like a child whose

pretty new toy has been taken away. He wanted her back, wanted her to sing, just for him. He just wanted her to sing.

He felt shy, suddenly, about approaching her. Could almost not believe he had sat with her in the rubble of Annie Trey's violated apartment, watching her smoke in the dark.

What was she doing in the dingy tenement? How did she create such a beautiful voice in a place like Cracker Village? And did he have the courage to ask her questions, now that he'd heard her sing?

The room closed in on him and he couldn't breathe. He stumbled to the door, generating stares. He made it out to the street, leaned up against the side of the building. The chipped brick felt rough and hot against his back, still warm with the accumulated heat of the day.

Listening to Valentine had loosened something inside him, something he'd just as soon not have touched.

He did not want to die. He did not want to be sick.

He looked up at the haze of yellow illumination spilling from the street light to the broken sidewalk. He hadn't done anything wrong. He had returned a child's teddy bear, and now he was sick. He could not sleep. If he did sleep, he woke up every hour, hot and cold and glistening with sweat. His throat hurt and his head ached, and it was all he could do to stay on his feet. He had no appetite. Food was the enemy people tried to force on him.

He wanted his life back the way it was before. He loved it all—his work, his ridiculous marriage, the little farmhouse that always needed work, the ragtag garden he neglected. His kids.

He had to be there to see them grow up. He had to.

He heard a soft footstep, the rattle of a pebble, a small sigh. He wondered if he was going to be murdered, or just robbed.

"Detective?"

He knew the voice instantly, of course. David turned around.

Valentine still wore the black dress, but the shoes dangled lazily from her fingers. She was barefoot, toenails painted blood-red. Her feet were surprisingly pretty—small,

nicely shaped, high arches and tiny toes. She crooked her
finger and David followed, going down a dirt pathway that
was choked with weeds, trash, and broken glass.

He did not warn her to watch her step or put on her
shoes—this was her territory; he was the stranger. And she
seemed charmed, moving languidly, eyes half closed. She
never made a misstep; her feet never touched the broken
glass, the trash, the rough, sawtoothed grass.

She stopped at the end of a low, crumbling brick wall
that ran parallel to the right side of the building. She
scooted to the top of the wall and perched there, legs swinging. David sat beside her, taking care not to come too close.
She was wearing perfume, David realized, something
heavy, woody, exotic.

Valentine lifted the hair off the back of her neck and
leaned into the muggy breeze.

"Did you come to hear me sing?"

"I can't think of a better reason."

She tilted her head and considered him. They stared at
each other for a long moment in the darkness. David heard
a car go by on the street.

She turned away finally, pointing to a tiny dirty window
that leaked harsh yellow light. "That's my dressing room,
right off the kitchen. Barely room in there to turn around,
and not as clean as I like."

David cleared his throat. "I had a million questions to
ask you, Valentine, but right now I can't think of a one."

She laughed softly. Music started up inside the club. David heard the chink of glassware, the rise and fall of voices.

"Something you wanted to know about our midnight
raid? About the *po*lice officers who weren't police officers,
who couldn't see in the light, and were pathetic when the
power went."

"What do you mean, couldn't see?"

"Just one of them, big guy, kept telling the others to
watch out for the toys, and then stepping on them himself.
He was clumsy. Walked into the wall, bumped into one of
the cabinets when the lights went out. I heard him swear."

"Did he wear a hat?"

"*Yes*—how'd you know that? You know who it is, David Silver police detective sir?"

"I might."

"A fellow brother police officer."

"This was no legitimate operation, Valentine."

"What's going on, Detective?"

"Why do I have the feeling you know more about it than I do?"

She scooted to the edge of the wall. "What would I know?"

"What do *you* think, Valentine? Do you think Luke Cochran is dead?"

She shrugged. "I don't really care about that, anyway."

"Didn't like him?"

"*Like* him?" She shook her head at David. "No. I didn't like him. Didn't hate him either. Just typical of the breed."

"Meaning?"

"For starters, look at Annie. Look how she lives. That baby boy was Luke's child too, but I didn't see him looking after Annie much. He cared more about that car than he did about her and little Hank, believe me."

"I do believe you. What happened that night, the night he disappeared?"

Valentine shrugged. "Just what Annie said. They were talking on the phone. He went down to see who was messing with his precious car. That's all we know."

"Annie didn't poison her baby," David said.

"I know."

"How do you know?"

"I know Annie."

David fiddled with the top button of his shirt. "Do you know Annie's social worker? Angie Nassif?"

"I don't like her, either."

"You see much of her?"

"Almost never. Not ever after Hank died. She came to the apartment once or twice, but mostly she liked to have Annie go to her office. Girl has to go through three bus exchanges to get there, but social workers are too important to come to us."

"You know who called in the complaint on Annie? Who started the ball rolling, investigating the baby's death?"

Valentine looked away. "I figured that was the social worker. Making trouble like they do."

"Somebody had to make a complaint."

She thought a minute. Shrugged one silk-clad shoulder. "Hospital, I guess, don't you think?"

David let it go. "You need a ride home?"

"I sing again in about an hour."

David looked into the field behind them, then back at her. "You want me to wait?"

She laughed at him. "Stay out of trouble, Detective. Go home to your wife."

It was, he realized, very good advice.

FORTY-FOUR

THURMON'S PRECINCT WAS ON THE OUTSKIRTS OF THE city, forty minutes in heavy morning traffic. It was mainly residential, down-at-the-heel degenerating middle class. A pasture for cops in their not-so-golden years, and younger screw-ups.

It was far enough out of the city's mainstream action that there was a parking lot beside the building, with empty slots. David gave the car directions and got out at the curb.

He had not slept after he left Valentine, but he'd had a shave, a shower, and a solid dose of Tylenol Twelve. He was sweaty again, and cold when he went through the double glass doors, past an ID scanner that dated back to 2025.

Not exactly top-of-the-line.

The furniture inside the precinct was old, with a cast-off, Salvation Army air. The carpet was grey and threadbare. Everything in the building had a tired, dingy air, and the smell made David think of retirement homes where the residents were reluctant and unhappy.

He clipped his ID to his belt, nodded at the woman who manned the booth.

"Thurmon, Missing Persons," he said.

She showed him two fingers and buzzed him through. He went to the elevator and waited, too tired to take the stairs to the second floor.

The elevator was slow, like everything else in the building. Thurmon was sitting behind his desk, chair pulled out, talking to two guys at desks across the room. A rubber-band whizzed through the air and landed in Thurmon's coffee cup, causing a small brown splash and an outbreak of laughter.

"Day-um—ten points, Larrimer. Don't drink that coffee, Thurmon."

"Hey, Stevie, even *I* saw that one. Hell of a shot, I'm buying, come lunch."

David stopped in front of Thurmon's desk, casting a shadow. "This the workload that kept you from following up that trouble with Annie Trey?"

The disapproval brought the room to immediate, uncomfortable silence. David didn't care. There were cops all over the city pulling double shifts, himself included. What justified keeping these guys on the payroll?"

Thurmon squinted at him, eyes milky, rimmed in red.

David leaned close. "It's Silver. David Silver."

"Yeah, I recognize you, I have *some* vision left. I was just wondering what makes you think you can walk in here and talk to me with that kind of attitude. I was a cop on the beat when you were still having your first—"

"Wet dream. Got you. Let me know when you're through taking a stand. Because we need to talk."

Thurmon leaned back in his chair, put his hat on his head, and angled it sideways with a practiced, theatrical motion.

"So talk."

David drummed his fingers on the edge of Thurmon's desk.

"Whatsa matter, kid? You got something to say, say it."

"You don't want to talk in private?"

"I got nothing to hide."

David nodded slowly, readying the bluff. "I checked before I came out here. Looks like six police flak jackets were missing from supply last—"

Thurmon stood up, face tight, eyes squinted into slits. "Maybe we should be private, Silver. Come with me."

They stood almost nose to nose in the janitorial supply closet. Thurmon clutched the edge of a shelf stacked with individually wrapped rolls of toilet paper. The room smelled like ammonia, soap, and, oddly, oatmeal.

Thurmon looked at him but didn't say a word. He was a smart cop, David realized, for all that he was out of the game. He wasn't going to give anything away for free.

"You wanted to talk, kid, now talk."

David folded his arms. "The one thing I don't know is what you were looking for when you beat down the door to Annie Trey's apartment, and scared those little girls so bad they don't sleep at night." It wasn't necessarily a lie. David had no real idea how the kids were doing. With any luck they'd bounced right back, but it sounded good. "Every night the littlest one wakes up crying, and the older one has gone back to sucking her thumb and won't eat. But, hey, Thurmon, they're just project kids, what the hell do you care?"

Thurmon's face went brick-red. "*I* grew up in the projects, Silver. Don't get high and mighty with me."

"Don't waste my time," David said. "Everything I ever heard about you said you were an okay guy who got a really bad deal. I never got any hint, before now, that you were dirty."

It was unexpected, and David was shaky anyway, so when Thurmon came after him with the sucker punch, he went down hard, landing up against a bench cluttered with empty soap boxes and work rags. He tried to get up, but the room was spinning and his legs were wobbly. He stayed down, lap full of dirty, sour rags, empty bucket by his head. He reached up for a handhold, which turned out to be a mop that clattered down across his legs. He felt a hand on his shoulder.

"Jeez, Silver, I'm sorry. You all right?"

"Been better."

"Can you get up?"

"Just need . . . a minute." He hated it, this breathlessness. It was a shock, the way his legs had gone out from under him. He wasn't sure he could make it to his feet. He was grateful for Thurmon's beefy hand under his elbow.

Thurmon cleared the bench with a swipe of a surprisingly heavily muscled arm, and settled David on the bench. David leaned back against the wall. He shut his eyes, chest tight, trying to catch his breath. He felt Thurmon unbutton the tight collar of his shirt, loosen the tie.

"Can I get you a glass of water, or a soda?"

David covered his mouth. Coughed. "Cup of coffee."

"You got it. Cream or sugar?"

One minute the man was slamming him into a wall, the next asking how he wanted his coffee. David laughed.

"What?"

"Nothing. Cream would be nice."

Thurmon was gone awhile, long enough for David's breathing to go back to normal, long enough for him to wipe blood from the corner of his mouth and straighten his tie. He could not remember being this embarrassed in years.

He heard footsteps. Thurmon came through the door, with a folding chair tucked under his right arm, coffee cup in his left hand. He handed David the mug of coffee. Steam shimmered wetly from the top.

"You look better, thank God. Be careful—I made a fresh pot, so it's hot."

Thurmon put the chair in the tiny space in front of the bench and closed the door. He sat down heavily. Shook his head at David.

"You've got it, don't you?"

"Got what?" David asked.

"The virus, or whatever the hell it is. The thing that killed that little Trey baby."

David nodded. "I've had a treatment. I'm not contagious."

"I won't say I'm not glad to hear it. Whatever it is, killed that baby in less than forty-eight hours."

David scratched his chin. "What about that raid at Annie's apartment? What were you guys after?"

Thurmon crossed his legs, flipped the tassel on top of his shoe. "We went in and got that teddy bear."

David looked at him. "They're not *that* valuable."

"No. But they're infected with the virus."

"How did you get in the middle of this, Thurmon?"

"Angie Nassif."

"The social worker?"

"Right. I've done things for her before. You know the drill. Get some off-duty cops, go to somebody's house, ask 'em to let us in. Nine people out of ten figure they have to; they don't know the law. That gets Angie in the door sometimes, when there's no other way it gets done.''

David had heard of this before, social workers with pet cops, who did off-duty favors.

"Hey, Silver, don't look like that. Angie does a lot of good, that girl. Helped a lot of kids.''

"Angie plays God,'' David said.

Thurmon shrugged.

"But why the big break-in? Why not just explain things to Annie, and tell her to give up the bear?''

"Hell, Angie tried. The kid didn't believe her. Said that the forensic lady, the Kellog woman, told her the bear couldn't be the source of infection. Annie thought Angie wanted the bear because it was valuable. Can't blame Annie, all the hell she's been through. She's not going to trust anybody. Especially not Angie.''

"So you went to all that trouble to get a teddy bear. You knew Annie wouldn't complain, and if she did, nobody would give a damn.''

"Miscalculated on that. There you sit.''

"Where did Annie get the bear in the first place?''

"Cochran. He got it from an antique dealer he worked for. She never would take money from him, not Annie. So it tickled him, made him feel like he put one over on everybody, to give her a bear worth that much.''

"How did you figure that out?''

"Angie told me. She knew Cochran. Look, Silver, I'm sorry about that raid. If I could go back and undo it, I would. Those little kids—'' He rubbed the back of his neck. "I'm not proud of myself, okay? But Angie was pretty convincing about the bear being a danger.''

"Where's the bear now?''

"Angie has it.''

FORTY-FIVE

THE PRECINCT WAS FLOODED WITH THE AROMA OF MICRO-
meals, and the spicy odor of takeout. Pizza, David decided,
and Chinese. The smells made him queasy. He had no appetite.

String breezed past him in the hallway. "Am to bring
the lunch, Detective David. Come soon for first choice."

David followed him into the bullpen. "Thanks, String, I
don't feel like tacos."

Della looked up and waved a hand. "Now what makes
you so sure he brought back tacos?"

Mel looked up from his computer. "Della, honey, String
always brings back tacos."

She looked at String. "What you got in the bag today?"

"The tacos, Della."

David went to his desk. Booted up his computer terminal
and checked for messages.

"Have heard from the Aslanti/Caper work team," String
said.

David looked up. "Is Aslanti working for the department
now?"

"Outside consultation, yes. And have done the bear to
bear analysis."

"What'd they find?" Mel said, without looking up.

"Bears most covered with the viral bacterium, but most
of them dead. Most hard to get infected this way, but possible. Aslanti feels there is a presence live host. You re-
members the night of finding car in Elaki-Town?" String
unwrapped a taco and took a small bite off the edge. David
grimaced at the smell of spicy meat and cinnamon. "Re-
members the noise I hear? Am sure I hear the predator
animal from home planet. Is called—"

"Trillopy," David said.

184

"Yesss."

"Aslanti told me trillopys are carriers."

String chewed another bite of taco. "Isss true this. Am checking to find if any have been smuggled in. Difficult this."

"And pointless," Mel said. "Assume it's here. Work from there."

David looked at Della. "You got that list I asked for?"

"In your reader, Silver. Why don't you look before you ask?"

"It's easier to ask." David rummaged in his center desk drawer for his reading glasses. His phone rang.

"Silver, Homicide."

"Hi, this is Tina Cochran, Luke's mother? Is this a bad time for you?"

David frowned. She sounded excited, upset. "Not at all, Mrs. Cochran. Is something the matter?"

"*No.* Yes. I . . . I don't know."

"What is? Tell me."

"I just got my mail. And I got . . . I got something in the mail from Luke."

David sat forward. "Are you sure it's from him? Do you recognize the handwriting?"

"Absolutely, it's his handwriting. And he had to have written it that Tuesday, the Tuesday he disappeared. That's the postmark. Plus it says 'when I saw you yesterday,' and I seen him that Monday before." Her voice went thick and David knew she was holding back tears. "I honestly don't know—I mean I'd like to think it shows he's alive. But I guess—I guess it really doesn't."

David kept his voice low-key and gentle. "Would you be willing to read me the note, Mrs. Cochran?"

David was aware that Della, Mel, and String were watching and listening. He felt self-conscious.

"You mean now?" Tina Cochran said.

David picked up a pen, grabbed a fresh scratch pad. "If you would. And it's important, Mrs. Cochran, not to leave anything out. Even if it seems . . . private."

"It says, 'Mama—I didn't say I love you yesterday when

I saw you. I can't even remember the last time I thanked you for all you've done for me, when I know times have been hard. I know you won't take my money, but maybe if I get a new, different kind of job, you'll take some of that. Anyway, I almost got killed tonight. It makes me think a lot. I've done something I'm not too proud of. So I'm writing you a note while I wait for the SART—you can see I had to scrounge for paper. You come close to death, Mama, it makes you think. I'm afraid I may be pretty sick. I'm planning to get well, but if I don't come over for a while, don't worry. I don't want you to catch this. Love, your son, Luke.' ''

She stopped reading and sobbed. David gave her a minute to get herself together.

"Mrs. Cochran, hang on to the note, will you? We're going to need to look at it."

"Oh. But . . . will I get it back?"

"I'll see that you do."

"It's . . . it's a good thing, isn't it?"

"I'm not sure what it means, long-term."

"It's like he's telling me he loves me. And it's kind of like . . . goodbye."

"Mrs. Cochran, are you all right?"

"I just—It's a funny thing, Detective. 'Cause I haven't give up hope all this time. And if you read the note, you could get from it that he was going to go away for a while. Kind of hide out. But . . .''

"But what?"

"Soon as I read it, I got the awfulest feeling. I think my boy is dead."

David didn't know what to say.

"Could you please just find out for sure, sir? One way or the other?"

David put his head in his hands. "I'll do my best, Mrs. Cochran."

"Bless you."

David hung up. Swore softly.

"What?" Della said.

David shook his head.

String hovered over his shoulder. "Isss this correct that she has communication from the dead?"

"He could still be alive," Della said.

"He was alive when he wrote it," David said.

"Maybe the yes, maybe the no." String swayed to one side. David waited for him to slide back in the other direction. He didn't.

"She recognize the handwriting?" Mel asked.

David nodded. He went to his reader, started the list while Mel picked up the note pad on his desk, passed it to Della.

Miriam's sister, Janet, had done a lot of shopping in the week since Miriam had been missing. She had bought clothes. Nothing definite there. A bathrobe. Makeup. David skipped to her grocery list.

Micro-meals, a lot of chicken, cat food, fiber bars, kiwi fruit, chewing gum, Coke, milk and ... David scrolled back. Orchard peach juice, chocolate bars, crunchy peanut butter.

So Miriam was alive. David chewed a knuckle, wondering how to find her. He picked up the phone to inquire when her sister went off shift.

FORTY-SIX

IT WAS DUSK WHEN DAVID AND MEL WATCHED JANET KEL-
log walk out of her precinct. She was striking in the black
uniform, body generously built and curvy, hair blond
enough to have come out of a bottle. Up close, her eyes
would be wide and blue. Two sisters could not have looked
less alike than Janet and Miriam.

"Maybe they *both* drink peach juice, ever think of that?"
Mel's voice was rough around the edges.

"Maybe."

"Reassure me, why don't you? And for the record, I still
think we should talk to Janet direct."

David was sleepy. He resisted the impulse to rest his
head against the car window. "Look, Mel, you called her
as soon as you got worried, right? And she said she hadn't
seen Miriam. She hasn't reported her sister missing, or
acted worried, and we know the two of them are close. If
Janet's telling the truth, talking to her won't help. If she
lied, it'll only put them on the alert."

"Them?"

"Janet and Miriam."

"I hope you're right about this, David."

"Me too. Okay, she's going. Don't get too close, but
don't lose her."

"Not a chance."

David was quiet while Mel drove. He looked at the tip
of white paper folded in Mel's right coat pocket. He'd seen
the hand-off, heard String say it was for him, David, from
Aslanti, but Della had flagged him down, and he hadn't
heard the rest of their conversation. He swallowed, throat
dry and hurting, wondered when Mel would see fit to hand
it over. Tried to decide whether or not he really wanted it.

"Shit," Mel said.

David realized he'd been dozing. He couldn't sleep at night if and when he ever got to bed, but let him sit still for a minute while he was working, and he couldn't keep his eyes open.

"She's going home."

"Park," David said.

"And then what?"

"Patience, Mel."

Mel pulled the car in across the street. They watched Janet go up the stairs to her town house, bend down as she opened the door and pick up a cat.

"What's that in your pocket, Mel? That for me?"

Mel looked at him, distracted. He patted his pocket, pulled the paper out. "Yeah, it's for you. From Aslanti."

"What is it, a bill?"

Mel's voice went low and offhand. "It's a list of symptoms. What you should look out for, so you know when to go to the hospital."

"You look at it?"

"Of course I looked at it. I'm nosy—I'm a cop, right? It's like this. You start feeling so crappy, you get dizzy spells and can't stay on your feet—that's like your clue. Go for help."

"Got ya."

Mel looked at him. "Isn't there *any*thing they can do?"

"Yeah. They're going to freeze-dry me at the hospital."

"Like a micro-meal?"

"They try and put me in a little square tray, I'm going home."

"You serious? They're really going to freeze-dry—"

"The virus and bacteria in my system. Just that part, we're hoping."

"Don't make assumptions when it comes to medics, David. They got methods of torture—Heads up, she's back."

"Told you. And would you mind not bringing up the words 'hospital' and 'torture' at the same time?"

"Aslanti will take care of you."

"Actually, I think she will. Okay. Stay on her."

"No back seat detective driving."

*   *   *

Janet led them across the city to the parking lot of the Continental Inn.

"I don't believe this. The *Continental*."

"Mel, it's the chic place to hide out."

"It's a *dump*."

"That too."

"Wasn't this where—"

David looked out the window. "Yeah. Yeah to whatever."

They both knew Mel meant Teddy. They both knew David didn't want to talk about it.

They hung back in the lobby. Janet had changed to jeans and a sleeveless denim shirt tied at the waist. She carried a bag that looked like it had groceries. She moved quickly without a backward glance, bypassed the elevators, and headed for the stairs.

Mel looked at David, who shrugged.

"We follow her. Miriam won't be registered under her own name. Janet will have to lead the way. Give her one second, to get ahead."

Mel bobbed up and down on the balls of his feet. "Jeez, I'm so nervous, my palms are sweating. That hasn't happened since—"

"Yesterday," David said.

Mel's grin was forced.

"Mel, there's something I want to mention about Miriam."

"Yeah? Come on, David, we don't want to lose Janet."

"Take it easy, don't get too close. Look, you should be prepared."

"For what?"

"Miriam may have . . . changed. Become more than . . . God, I sound stupid."

"You got that right." Mel opened the swinging door to the stairwell, and David followed him in.

Janet was waiting for them on the third step, feet apart, gun at the ready—police issue, glowing green from her fingerprints, safety off.

"You?" she said.

"Hi," David said.

"Hi? What the hell are you guys doing here?"

"Following you."

"That I know. I wasn't sure, but I had a funny feeling when I was driving over."

"*No* way you made us," Mel said.

"But I definitely picked you up in the lobby. Wished I'd turned around to get a look at you. Would have saved me sitting on these damn stairs with my hands shaking. I was afraid the gun would go off before you got here."

"What a shame that would be," Mel said. "Speaking of which."

But Janet had already thumbed the safety back on, and was sliding the gun into her purse. In spite of her words, David noticed that she handled the weapon with an offhand authority that he envied.

"What are you doing here, guys?"

Mel sighed. "Don't be conversational, Janet. I been worried sick. I want to see her."

"She's been wanting to see you. I talked her out of it."

"Thank *you* so very much."

"I'm trying to keep her safe, and it's hard as hell to figure out what's going on."

"Hey, we're on the case and we got no idea."

"Time we compared notes," David said.

FORTY-SEVEN

IF DAVID HAD HARBORED ANY DOUBTS ABOUT MEL AND Miriam, they vanished when Miriam opened the door and saw Mel in the hallway.

Her mouth opened, her eyes lit up. He held out his arms and she went to him. David looked at Janet.

"Sickening, isn't it? David and I are going on in, guys. Under the circumstances, I think PDA's in the hallway are a *really* bad idea." Janet sat on the edge of the bed and patted a spot next to her. "Get off your feet, my friend, you looked whipped. Miriam, for God's sake, close the door and lock up."

Miriam closed the door and locked it and led Mel to the bed. She scrambled into the middle as unselfconsciously as a kitten and tugged Mel's hand so he'd sit beside her.

"Ain't this nice," Janet said.

David was struck by how much she sounded like Mel.

Miriam gave her a look. "I told you he'd find me. I wanted to call you, Mel, but we decided it wasn't safe. You must have been worried sick."

"Not for a minute."

"He was beside himself." David looked at his partner. Mel seemed years younger all of a sudden, and his voice was lightweight. Definitely a goner. Wedding bells, David thought. Which, under the circumstances, wasn't such a bad idea.

He glanced surreptitiously at Miriam. She wore cutoff jeans that were strained at the waist. The slight swell of belly was there if you knew to look for it. Strange to think the child inside was his future niece or nephew.

Mel plucked at the sleeve of her loose cotton shirt. "I wondered where that shirt got to."

She grinned. Then sobered. "I have a million things to

tell you, but I'm starving. Anybody else hungry?''

Janet shrugged.

Mel pursed his lips. ''Now that you mention it. They don't have room service here, do they?''

Janet rolled her eyes. ''The man is an optimist or an idiot. Never fear, guys, she's got a stash you would not believe.''

Miriam stuck her tongue out, wriggled off the bed, and burrowed in the small, dingy refrigerator. She passed around a bucket of cold barbecued chicken nuggets, mango strips, chocolate bars, and a jar of peanut butter. She was drinking Orchard peach juice, but Janet, mercifully, came up with an eight-pack of beer.

''*One* of us isn't—'' She stopped abruptly, looked from Miriam to Mel. ''Never mind.''

Mel took a swallow of beer. ''One of you isn't what? Pregnant?''

Miriam, settled again in bed, took her finger out of the jar of peanut butter that, oddly enough, no one else seemed interested in sharing. ''Mel. You know?''

''Either you're pregnant or you've spent the last couple of weeks eating everything in sight. Looks like both to me.''

''If I felt like getting up, I'd hit you,'' Miriam said flatly. ''When did you figure it out?''

''Not till you went missing. I started telling David about you one morning, kind of adding things up, while he was feeding his pet pig.''

Janet looked at David. ''He *did* say 'pig'?''

Mel kept talking. ''And he gets this real funny look. Then he starts dropping all these heavy hints, so I talked it over with Della, and she told me in three minutes flat you were pregnant.''

''Well?''

''Well? Well, why didn't you tell me?''

''Here they go,'' Janet said.

''I wasn't sure how I felt about things.''

''Yeah, I found that list you made. You like my butt, but you're afraid I may be set in my ways.''

David moved off the bed to a chair, mainly for the back support, though it wouldn't hurt to be out of the line of fire. He was tired. He wanted to go home. He closed his eyes.

"David?" Mel was tapping his shoulder. "David?"

He opened his eyes, got the feeling that time had passed. He rubbed the back of his neck. His head hurt. It was an effort to sit up in the chair.

"Sorry. I fall asleep?"

Mel looked at him. "You had anything at all to eat today?"

"I ate earlier."

"Sure you did."

"Mel. Leave it. Miriam, I need to hear what happened the night Cochran disappeared, if you and Mel have settled your personal business. Is Luke dead?"

Miriam stood up, one knee on the bed. David couldn't help remembering Teddy in a room just like this one—Teddy eating pizza, watching basketball, reading her romance books. Making love. He wished that he could talk to her. That she would call.

Miriam's voice had gone down an octave. She sounded professional, serious. "I wish I knew, David. I was on my way out the door when I got Annie's message, so I called her back. But Angie Nassif answered the phone and . . . what?"

"The social worker," David said. "So she was at Annie's that night?"

Miriam nodded. "Annie was doing something with the baby, so that Nassif woman picked up the phone. Not my favorite person. I needed to see Luke, so I decided to go to his place first. He's in the dorms, so it was on my way."

"Why see Luke?" Mel asked.

"I wanted to talk to him about the teddy bear. And I think he had whatever it was that killed Annie's baby. He'd been sick for a while and was getting sicker. I wanted to test him."

"She's scared to death she'll get it," Janet said.

"It's not serious for women," David said.

"What about pregnant ones?" Mel asked.

Miriam put a hand on her belly and bit her bottom lip.

"Good move," David said. "Keep talking, Miriam. What happened when you saw Luke?"

"I parked my car, and heard voices, saw Luke arguing with three Elaki, right next to that car of his. So I went over and . . . They were formidable. The Elaki. And well-armed. They, um, they made Luke get in the car. And they stuffed *me* in the trunk!" She sounded indignant, but David heard the quiver underneath.

"I was sure they were going to kill him, and then me. They were . . . they were angry. Hard-acting. I don't know how to explain it, but those guys meant business. I figured if I waited till they let me out, I was dead anyway. So I found this crowbar and tore my way into the back seat of the car."

Janet was shaking her head. "You believe this?"

Mel tried to smile. "Tough girl."

Miriam chewed the end of her reddish-brown hair. "It wasn't hard, guys—there's really nothing but fabric and insulation on that model car. I heard shouting and . . . Luke was bleeding, struggling with one of the Elaki. I started hitting them." She rubbed her face with her hands. "The driver got distracted; he was turned around, trying to help and I kept hitting with the crowbar. I figured my only chance was to cause a car wreck, but try getting a driver screwed up enough to get a car off-track."

"It worked," David said.

She gave him a grim look. "Yeah. Right at the Elaki-Town exit. We went over that guardrail into the weeds, and the next thing I know, we're surrounded by an Elaki mob." She shivered. "It was so weird. They were kind of quiet, but *there*. Like, pulsing with rage. About half of them had their backs turned, and the others didn't." She laughed harshly. "And some of them couldn't make their minds up, so they kept doing their little circle dance." She took a breath. "It was damn scary. There were so *many* of them. Luke was dazed—he had some cuts—and they dragged him out of the car. They were rougher with him than me.

"I thought I was dead, I really did. And then this Elaki comes out of nowhere like the Lone Ranger. Wades right into the crowd. He was so . . . so calm, but, I don't know, he had presence. And energy. I'm not explaining it right."

"Charisma," Mel said.

"Everybody listened to him. He even made them laugh a couple times, which, believe me, was amazing. He diffused things. But he argued too. They all talked fast, and I couldn't understand. I know he pointed to me a couple of times. But whatever they said, he wouldn't back down. I thought they were going to kill all three of us.

"Then, I don't know what he said, maybe something like 'shame on you.' He turned his back on them. So, before he's like standing in front of me, like a shield. And now he's facing me. And he's talking real soft, and I realize he's talking to me in English. It took me a minute. I was . . . stunned, I don't know. Not exactly on top of things.

"And he says to me . . . 'Are they turning their backs?' And I realize that's what they're doing. And he says, 'Can you walk about a half mile, if your life depended on it?' I nodded at him, like a dork, and he kind of politely wants to know if I mean yes by the head bobbing, and I say, 'Yes.' So he says soon as all the backs are turned, go down the ramp and go left and don't look back. And there'll be a taco stand called One-Eyed Jacks, and to tell the Elaki there that Sifter Chuck said for them to take me anywhere I want to go, and to do it fast."

"Then what?" Mel said.

"That's what I did."

"Where'd you go?"

"Bus stop. I didn't want anybody to know where I went. I called Janet and came here. Been here ever since."

"Why didn't you call me?" Mel said.

"It was a blood sanction kind of deal, Mel. Best if everyone thinks I'm dead. I didn't know if Luke was killed or not. If he was, then obviously I'm next. There are Elaki all through the department. If I call, even if they don't know where I am, they're going to start watching Janet. Which puts her and me in that much more danger. If you don't act worried and look for me, same thing. What *did* happen to Luke?''

''We don't know,'' David said.

FORTY-EIGHT

THEY HAD WAITED SUPPER FOR HIM, ROSE AND HIS LITTLE
girls, though it was late to be eating dinner, and a school
night at that. Kendra had cooked homemade mashed potatoes.

David forced down the food and smiled at his daughters.
They were up too late, and wound up tight, so they carried
the conversation with a great deal of noise and enthusiasm.
A good thing. David was too tired to talk.

Afterwards, they left the dishes in the sink, and Rose and
David sat on the stoop of concrete that made up the back
porch.

He noticed a small green tomato plant coming up by the
edge of the porch. He knew he hadn't put it there. He
looked around the yard. It was not his imagination; produce
was coming up, albeit in random locations. The dog had
not eaten his plants, she'd just moved them. There was a
time when the disorder would have made him crazy, but
he smiled inwardly. He would take his garden as it came.

Rose squeezed his hand. "So Miriam is okay?"

David looked at her, startled.

"Mel called and told me."

"Rose, I'm sorry. I can't believe I forgot to tell you."
He was cold, but the heat was starting up, and he dreaded
the fluttery, tight panic in his chest. Within seconds, he had
broken a sweat. How could he have forgotten to tell her?
Was his mind going?

"David, you want to go to bed, it hurts to look at you."

"Don't look at me."

They were interrupted, mercifully, by the slamming of
the back door, and a parade of children fresh and clean
from their baths, ready for bed and bearing gifts.

198

Lisa beckoned to Mattie, who put a box wrapped in gold foil at their feet.

"Open it."

David looked at Rose. "You."

She gave the girls her sideways, playful look. David had not seen that look in ages.

"It's dirty socks," Rose said.

"Pig chow," David guessed.

The foil revealed a cardboard box. Rose lifted the top.

"Because you broke all the dishes," Kendra said.

Rose laughed. David peered into the box. Paper plates, plastic cups. He smiled and gave his daughters extra long hugs, but he got the message. Rose herded the girls off to bed.

Mattie lagged behind. "Daddy. Can you read the story tonight?"

He wanted to pick her up, but he didn't have the strength.

Rose's voice came in through the screened door, saying Daddy didn't feel good, so give him an extra kiss and come on.

She knew the right things to say to make it all better for the children, David thought.

He missed Teddy. He wanted to talk to her. Sometimes he touched the phone and said her name, but he was kidding, because he had no intention of picking it up. What if he died and never saw her again?

He had waited too late. He closed his eyes, wishing she would call him, imagining the phone ringing, himself saying hello. But all the time he imagined it, he knew it wasn't going to happen.

FORTY-NINE

HE HAD GONE TO SLEEP THINKING OF TEDDY, SO WHEN THE
phone rang, he was sure it was her.

It was Dispatch.

"Detective Silver, sorry to disturb you, but we've had
an emergency call from the home of Angela Nassif. Do
you know a young woman named Crystal?"

David sat up. "Yes."

"I'm sorry, sir, the situation is a little . . . What I know
is we've got blood trails and a young woman who seems
very shocky. She refuses to talk to anybody. She asked for
you. We thought—"

"I'll be right there."

Rose propped herself up on one elbow. Her eyes were
dark with exhaustion. He wasn't the only one not sleeping.

"Want me to drive you in?" she asked.

She was good, David thought. No questions, just pure
practicality.

"No thanks," he said.

The street looked different at night, busy with patrol cars,
and an ambulance poised and waiting. The uniforms had
cordoned off Angie Nassif's yard as well as the one next
door. David thought about blood trails.

He sent his car to find a spot farther down the block,
walked up to the unmarked car. A woman in sensible shoes
turned, looked at him as he clipped his ID to the waistband
of his jeans.

He saw from the ID on her grey blazer that she was
Sergeant Courtney.

"You're Silver?"

He nodded.

"Good of you to come. Look, I know you're here to talk

to this girl, but you better get grounded first. It's a mess."
She headed for the open front door without a backward
glance, and he dutifully followed.

The first thing he noticed, after the blood, was the sliding
glass doors open, curtains torn and pulled away. Moths,
drawn by the light and possibly by the smell of blood, had
congregated on the ceiling. A pink dress-shoe lay on its
side by the couch.

"You have any idea what happened?" David asked.

"Obviously from the blood and tissue, somebody was
fatally attacked. How exactly . . . kind of hard to imagine
at this point. I'm assuming the attacker used something big
and sharp, maybe a machete." She pointed to the overturned couch, the broken lamp. "There are parts over
there."

David took a quick look. Saw two toes, still connected,
lying next to a blood spattered barbell. The severed edge
of the toes was ragged, the flesh torn. Not clean enough for
a machete, David thought.

"God," he muttered.

"Yes. Sorry to drag you into this."

"It's okay." He focused on her face, the nicest thing to
look at in this room. She'd be close to retirement, black
hair liberally streaked with grey, small half-glasses on her
nose. A bit on the thin side, David thought. Worked long
hours, skipped meals.

She moved in an aura of energy and competence he
found attractive.

"Where's the body?" If Crystal had asked for him, it
had to be Angie who was dead.

Sergeant Courtney grimaced. "This way. Trail starts
here."

The blood glistened wetly on the carpet. David followed
the dark line out the sliding doors onto the small patio and
into the grass. The blood-soaked mate to the pink shoe had
caught in a crack between patio tiles.

The smears of blood thinned and widened. The grass was
torn and scuffed.

"Dragged?" David asked.

"Yes. Look at this."

The yard was fenced in by an eight-foot wood privacy job. One of the planks had come loose and sagged to one side. Someone or something had forced their way through, splintering the wood. Bits of tissue and blood were clotted on the jagged edges. A snag of material—pink cotton— hung limply from one of the broken slats.

"Nasty, isn't it?" Courtney said.

David followed her to a back gate that hung open. The other side of the fence was bordered with a flower garden, thick with begonias. Humped up against the fence where the wood had broken through was what was left of Angie Nassif.

She had not changed out of her work clothes—stayed late at the office, perhaps. Both lapels of her pink blazer were slippery and red. She was on her back, cushioned by pink and white blossoms, face up, unfortunately. Her legs were bent and twisted, one foot mangled, and her right wrist ended in a well of blood.

David wondered where they'd find the hand. Or if they'd find it.

She had been disemboweled, stomach torn open, ropy coils of intestine spilling over the sides. David asked Courtney for a light, and shined it into the open body cavity.

He looked up. "Not a machete."

"Yeah, it would be clean cuts and these aren't. This one's really got me rattled."

David switched off the light. "She's been mauled. Looks like whatever tore her up was feeding. There are . . . parts missing. Internally. And smears of blood here, around the ribs."

Courtney shook her head. "But what—a lion, do you think? Because if so, we need to get people dispatched to catch this thing."

David hesitated. He hated interdepartmental secrecy, because it put people at risk.

"I think it's a trillopy."

"A *what*?"

"It's an Elaki thing."

"But—"

"Smuggled in someway—I don't know how yet, but I will."

"How did—"

"I'm sorry, Sergeant Courtney. I really don't have any useful details. I've never even seen one of these things. I just know they're predators and, clearly, dangerous as hell. If you have an Elaki advisor, give him a call. And, this is important, Sergeant—the animal may be infected with a potentially lethal viral bacterial hybrid. For all I know, the corpse may be contaminated. Have your people take precautions."

She shook her head. "You *look* sane."

"This is complicated. It's tangled up with a missing person case that's turning into a homicide."

"Why do I have the distinct feeling you may be in hot water for telling me this?"

David shrugged. "Your people need to be protected, and they should know what they're up against. And the water is already as hot as I hope it gets."

A shiver went through the sergeant, sudden and involuntary.

David had only looked at Angie Nassif's face for a moment or two, but the afterimage stayed in his mind.

"Crystal," he said.

"Follow me."

FIFTY

CRYSTAL WAS UPSTAIRS IN HER ROOM, SITTING STIFFLY ON the edge of the bed. David was reminded of the way Kendra looked in the dentist's office. Crystal seemed miraculously composed, not necessarily a good sign. There was no color in her face.

David noticed a backpack peeking out from under the bed. Some of the dresser drawers were partly open. Crystal wore a jacket, sturdy shoes, hair braided back. Dressed for the road, David thought.

He knew better than to try and touch her. He took a small white chair from behind an imitation French Provincial desk, and pulled it halfway across the room, facing her. Close, but not too close.

"Hello, Crystal."

When she smiled, she looked very young. She put her hands in the pockets of the jacket. It was hot in the room, but she was shocky, she'd be cold.

"I'm not going to the hospital."

He knew the feeling. "They can't make you."

"They'll try."

David looked pointedly at the backpack. "But you'll be gone by then."

She tilted her head. Spoke softly. "Are you going to tell on me?"

He shook his head. "I don't think you should just take off, Crystal, I don't think you should be alone, but it's up to you. Is there anyone you can go to?"

"No, sir."

"Not *any*one?"

"*No* sir."

"I could put you up for a while. I live on a farm, you could help me with the animals. I've got a pig, a dog and a cat, a cow that eats candy.''

She smiled, but it was a *no*. Her face went soft and sweet while she'd thought about the animals. She could have been a happy child, David thought, if she'd had the chance.

"I've been on the road before, Mr. Silver. I know how to handle myself. I know where all the right shelters are.''

"Crystal, there are people who will help you.''

She gave him a look that was wise, old, and knowing. "I've been part of that system all my life. It's a hard way to live and I wouldn't wish it on my worst enemy.''

David reached into his pocket, pulled out a magnetic card he kept for emergencies. "Free credit. Unattached, payable to bearer. Don't lose it.''

She took it with a grateful look, made it disappear inside the jacket. "Thank you.''

They were quiet while she contemplated the floor.

"I have a lot of important stuff to tell you.''

"Can you talk now?''

"Now or never.'' Her voice went softer, and very flat. "Angie worked late tonight, so I fixed supper. I set the table and was cooking micro-meals. I was busy, so she . . . she took the bearfox outside to do its business. I was afraid of it, so she always took care of it.''

"Bearfox?''

"I forget what it's really called. She got it from the Elaki.''

David could swear she was telling the truth. Could Angie Nassif really be so stupid? "Are you talking about a trillopy?''

"Yeah, that's it.''

"You kept it here?''

"Angie did. She got it one night, a few days ago. It was going to be evidence to clear Annie Trey.'' Crystal looked David in the eye. "Annie didn't kill that baby, it got sick. Angie said the bearfox . . . the trillopy, would prove it, because the animal carried the sickness.'' Her eyes widened. "They were going to take Jenny away from her mother. The motion thing was already in effect, so Angie said she had to cut corners and work real fast. The teddy bear thing didn't turn out, and Angie was real disappointed. But the bear was worth a lot of money. She was going to sell it and quit her job and we were going away to be safe.'' Crystal bit her lip. ''Sometimes I think there's nowhere safe in this world.''

''Crystal—''

She shook her head. ''Angie was real worried about this thing with Annie, and didn't want to leave till it was settled. She quit sleeping, just worried worried worried. Then one night she goes out and comes back with this trillopy thing. She said it was trained to be a pet and wouldn't hurt us if we were careful. I was scared of it. But Angie would pet it, and it licked her hand.''

David had a sudden image of Angie's wrist, smeared with blood.

''I was in the kitchen when I heard her start screaming. She sounded mad and real scared. I ran to the living room. The sliding glass door was open, and there was another one in the yard.''

''Another trillopy?''

Crystal nodded.

''And this one wasn't a pet,'' David said.

Crystal stared at the floor. ''It was real big, the other one. It wasn't acting like any animal I ever saw before. I think it came for the female. It . . . I think the female may have been in season. Like dogs?''

David nodded at her to continue. He had no idea.

''That's kind of how it was acting.'' Her face was pinking up. At least it had color. ''Angie had ours on a chain, and she . . . she wouldn't let it go. She tried to drag it back in. She was so . . . *stubborn*.''

Stupid, David would have said, but didn't. He waited for Crystal to tear up and break down. She didn't. Her face, if possible, went blander and her voice was a monotone, with no emotion in it.

''Then the big one went for her. I think she knew then, she'd done a dumb thing. She screamed for me to run. She got back inside, but the big one was mad, it came in with her, and I don't think she even knew that she still had the chain on the little one. I kept yelling at her, drop the leash, drop the leash. But then . . . then it got her. So I ran away.'' Crystal wrapped her arms around her chest. ''I thought it would come get me. I heard it. Her screaming and crying and making bubbles in her throat.''

''There was nothing you could do, Crystal. You handled yourself very well.''

She shrugged. ''I threw the coffeepot at it and it didn't hardly notice. I had to run away. No use us both being dead.''

''It was Angie's mistake and it killed her.''

Crystal nudged the backpack with the back of her heel and looked up at David. ''I know why, though. She was so scared about Annie Trey. She felt really guilty.''

David frowned. ''Why guilty?''

''I never could really figure that out.''

''Do you know who made the complaint about Annie? Who got the investigation started?''

''Oh, yeah. Because that's why Angie was so worried. Because it was Luke Cochran.''

David didn't move or say a word. Luke Cochran? Something here he didn't want to know. Something he didn't want to face.

Crystal kept talking. ''She said he used her, and he used Annie, and it was really bad what he did, and she was going to see about it.'' Crystal leaned toward him, almost touching. ''She didn't want Annie and her little girl getting chewed up in the system. And, Mr. Silver, I want to ask you please not to let that happen. I saw that little girl's picture in the paper. She's soft. Not like me. It would be really bad for her, really bad.''

Crystal's eyes were tearless. David knew that the minute his back was turned she would be lost to the streets of the city. And all he could think of was that she was soft, too.

It came to him that she might be infected, and he could not let her go.

FIFTY-ONE

DAVID DID NOT KNOW WHAT HE WAS RUNNING ON—
adrenaline, anger, general contrariness. Sifter Chuck was
home. There were lights shining from the second floor, and
the pulse of loud music.

David beat on the door a second time, this go-round with
his fists.

There were lights on all over Elaki-Town, a good sign.
Very few Elaki out, but the ones he saw gave him long
looks. He understood now what Miriam had meant when
she said the crowd was quiet but pulsing with rage.

He stepped away from the shuttered doorway, looked in
the gutter for loose gravel. He found a chunk of asphalt
and chucked it into the well-lit window.

"*Sifter!* Open up."

The asphalt connected, and glass shattered. He hadn't
meant to throw it quite so hard.

Sifter Chuck appeared at the window.

"*Sifter.* It's Silver."

The Elaki disappeared. Lights came on downstairs, and
the door opened. Sifter slid partway out, belly rigid.

"Isss drunken, stupid, or naive beyond belief?"

"How about pissed as hell."

Sifter pushed the door wide. "Get you in, and keep the
voices down."

David scooted in. The music was loud. Antique bears
displayed on the wall wobbled along with the bass.

"There are questions that become urgent for a late-night
fool risk?"

David leaned against the wall. "I'm tired, you understand me? I feel like hell, and I am out of patience with
you. Listen up and no bullshit."

The Elaki began to sway.

"Be still and turn down that music. No, stay, we don't have time. Look. I *know* there are trillopys in the city. You understand I'm not guessing, I know. My guess is they were smuggled in with your bears, because the bears are lousy with dead bacteria and the trillopys are diseased. Two of them are loose. We've had one victim already, torn to pieces. Now we've got the animals running around spreading this virus. Talk to me now, or I'll throw you to the Feds. God knows what they'll do to you, but your teddy bear days will be over, and you'll never find the elusive Pez."

"What be the wants?"

"Where are the trillopys? How many are there?"

Sifter considered him, going still in the mode of serious Elaki agitation. "Have car?"

"Yes."

"Please to transport.

"Okay. But my head hurts. Don't even think about turning on the radio."

FIFTY-TWO

THE REILLY HOTEL HAD THE MOST BEAUTIFUL POOL DAVID
had ever seen, though the Elaki would most certainly refuse
to use it. The pool was a leftover from the old days when
the hotel catered to humans, and it was still maintained with
the kind of reverential and meticulous care engendered by
limitless funds.

David stared through the slatted wood fence. The water
moved gently in the darkness, lit from the sides, ripples
like a web of wrinkles skimming the restless turquoise surface. Fig trees lined the square white tiles up and down the
sides of the pool. Even at night, the white umbrellas were
open. They looked more like frilly feminine parasols than
poolside umbrellas. In the afternoon they would shade the
bamboo chairs and tables that were grouped attractively by
the water.

On the left was a green-tiled Jacuzzi. It bubbled softly,
heat rising. On the right, up three marble steps, was a
shaded terrace and bar. The floor was cool grey slate, the
ends bordered by achingly white columns. The entire hotel
had a British colonial look that was graceful, elegant,
inviting.

It surprised him, how badly he wanted to swim in that
pool. The water made him feel thirsty. It shamed him,
somehow, that no matter how much money he had, he
would never be allowed to swim quietly up and down,
never be allowed to sit under the pretty umbrellas, never
be allowed to sit in one of the rattan chairs on the terrace
and order something cold to drink.

David was relieved when Sifter returned. He had
been warned that they were on shaky ground. He had been
warned that they were dealing with a powerful diplomat

who, however he might be in the wrong, wielded influence they could only guess at.

Sifter led him across a terrazzo floor, the Elaki gliding gracefully, bottom fringe swept sideways. They passed through the white arches, clean and white and impossible. David smelled chlorine from the pool, then they passed through swinging doors into a well-lighted corridor. David could see an Elaki approaching from the other side.

Sifter stopped, holding a fin out. David stopped too and waited, aware that there were courtesy issues involved.

The Elaki moved slowly, like a state procession, and though he was bent to one side, ever so slightly, his bearing was dignified without overreaching into the arrogant land of regal.

The Elaki slid to a stop. Looked David over for a long, silent moment, making David conscious that he had thrown on his jeans and shirt, that he'd be better off with a shower.

The Elaki raised a fin in a motion that was languid and somehow dismissive. "You are the law type official?"

David showed his ID. "I'm a detective with the Saigo City Police Department."

"You will be good to walk with me slowly, and listen to what I am saying. This will meet with you approval, yes?"

David nodded and fell into pace with the Elaki. He was quite an elder, this one. His inner belly coloring had faded, his scales lacked luster, and he could not straighten up. He moved with the slow care of the aged or the impossibly lazy, but the pace suited David. He was not well.

"I am last of my chemaki. You understand significance, this?"

David was aware of Sifter Chuck, sliding along behind them. He nodded. In human terms, the man had no family.

"What I do have is long-lived companion you know as trillopy. I have the awareness that this bond is seen as indulgence. You would call her a pet." The Elaki was quiet a minute. "She is domesticated and gives the affectionate companion time. My attachment, however you see the big picture, sir, is genuine and strong. When asked to serve in capacity of diplomatic service, I am tired. But needed. Quite simply, I could not bear to leave her behind. I am assure she is not the threat.''

"That makes three trillopys by my count, sir. Why so many?''

"One alone cannot survive without at least one other. Must have physical presence of others in species. Three is sum total, I do assure.''

"Are all of them infected?'' David was prepared to be lied to.

"My special girl is ailing with this disease. Not just a carrier she, but very sick. At first sign of symptoms, all split and quarantined. I do not believe others have the active infection, but to be fully disclosed, must admit to the possibility.''

They turned a corner. David smelled animal smells, and a peculiar musky odor he associated with sickness.

"What were you thinking to let Angela Nassif take a trillopy with her?''

"One she takes is also domesticated. Safe enough with careful handling. Unusual also in the goodness of nature— offborn of my own special girl.''

"Still.''

"She does not give me much choice, this Nassif. She will take one, or demand all be taken away, and destroyed. The deal is she will hold off just the short while mine takes to finish end of life. My pet will die soon, and I wish to keep my own special girl with me till the end. She needs to stay with gentle handler me, for quality of last hours.

"I give to Nassif the healthy female, and feed her belief, possibly false, that all such species are carriers, and for her purpose interchangeable. But this female is seasonal. This mean—''

"I know what it means,'' David said.

"We have underestimate the drive of the male. Break away from confinement. Iss loose. And, as you have told Sifter, finds mate.''

David grimaced, wondering if there was now a pregnant

trillopy running around Saigo City, thanks to this self-indulgent old Elaki.

"Here she be."

The trillopy had a chain on its hind foot, chain wrapped in velvet with a long lead. Crystal was right, it did look like a bizarre mating between a bear and a fox. It was four-legged, with a long, narrow snout and close-set eyes.

If it stood up, it would be waist-high. This one was not standing up.

It lay on its side, nestled in a thermal cotton blanket, yellow against the mahogany fur. The eyes were round, brown flecked with yellow. David looked into the face of the beast and saw how very sick and miserable it was.

He wished Rose was here. Though she would likely side with the Elaki.

The trillopy could not have much longer to live. The old Elaki slid down sideways, careless, graceless, and stroked a fin across the animal's dull, lusterless fur. The female was perilously thin, and her breath came hard and fast.

David could not stop staring at the animal, thinking it was the origin of the disease that was killing him. The trillopy made a mewing trill, high-pitched and wavering with distress, and David felt his anger drain away.

FIFTY-THREE

ONCE DAVID FOLLOWED THE SCENARIO TO ITS LOGICAL conclusion, things began falling in place.

He parked, took the shovel he'd found resting behind the barn, and left the car in the parking lot at the Bailey Farmstead.

Suppose, just for the sake of argument, Luke Cochran survived the confrontation with the Elaki-Town mob, thanks to the efforts of Sifter-Chuck. Then what? Where would he go? What would he do?

He'd head home to his girl, Annie Trey. Or, if he was scared, he might ask her to meet him somewhere. Somewhere off the beaten path, where there were no Elaki, where he wouldn't be seen. He'd had an epiphany of sorts, brought on by his brush with death, and was considering mending his ways. He even dropped a note to his mother.

David walked slowly across the lawn toward the forest, pacing himself. He was distracted, imagining the scene in his head.

If Luke expects to be welcomed with open arms, he is to be sorely disappointed.

Annie has found out, thanks to Angie Nassif. Annie might forgive him for bringing the infection that overwhelmed her newborn baby's tiny and immature immune system, sweeping him away. Surely it was unintentional, if tragic. But then Luke set off the wolfpack, lodged a complaint that held this impossibly young unwed mother of two up to public vilification. She was Southern and poor and uneducated. She lived in the projects. She brought out the smug intolerance of people who liked a target that could not fight back.

David paused at the tree line, looking for the path. His breathing was already labored, fast and irregular. He rested

214

a while, letting his heartbeat slow, the tightness in his chest ease up. He lodged the dull metal blade of the shovel against his shoulder, and went slowly down the path, wondering why.

Luke would not have lasted long in any competent investigation. Illegal Elaki animals smuggled into the city would cause enormous problems for a certain powerful Elaki diplomat, particularly when it became clear that the animals had gifted the human race with yet another killer disease. Perhaps the diplomat had been very grateful. David thought of Luke's gleaming black car.

Had Luke realized what the outcome would be, when he made the accusation? Did he even suspect that Annie would twist in the wind on the five o'clock news, that Social Services would close in on Jenny, and take her away? Was this really nothing more than a romance gone wrong, a lover getting back at his girlfriend?

Men had a history of relationship intolerance. Things women accepted, however bitterly, drove men to pick up a gun.

David's steps got slower and slower, and he did not think about distance, so he was surprised when he found himself back where he'd fallen asleep against the tree.

The sun had been up less than an hour, and the morning was mercifully cool. The rainfall had been good for that, at least.

Something had bothered him, that other night, digging up the bear by the barn. Recognition—of what he'd been too ill to remember. But it had come to him in the dark, quiet hours, when he was the only one in the world still awake, too miserable and tired to sleep.

He had seen it before, the wide, mature girth of a tree, decades old, flanked by thin, gangling juniors. The soft light of morning turned the leaves almost turquoise. The tree was scarred down the middle, bark stripped bare. It was here that Annie had painted a red and yellow flame, when she'd painted the scene on the nursery wall where little Hank's mobile should have been.

The dirt at the base of the tree was crumbly and humped,

and had obviously been disturbed. David flipped the shovel over, and started to dig.

It took two hours, moving slowly, with frequent breaks and sweat streaming down his face and back, but he found it, ironically close to their dig the other night.

First a hand, streaked with dirt, the cuff of the shirt sleeve missing one button. David wondered if Luke had been uncomfortable, wearing a long-sleeved shirt in this heat. His own sleeves were rolled high on his arms, and sweat ran down his biceps and dripped on the ground. His palms stung where perspiration leaked over the white bubbles of blisters that rose, cupped in angry red flesh.

He stopped to put on a mask, thinking it would be nice if he'd remembered to bring gloves.

It was a stroke of luck, uncovering the top of the torso right off. It saved a lot of digging. Cochran was on his back, eyes, open mouth, nostrils and ears all leaking loose black dirt. The smell of him rose like a tangible thing, and David gagged. The body was damp and sloppy, decomposing fast in the heat. He could not tell by looking how she'd done it.

David decided he wanted time to think. He gave Cochran one last, quick look, then began piling the dirt back on.

He wondered if Annie had had any help.

FIFTY-FOUR

WHEN DAVID LOOKED AT ANNIE TREY, HE SAW THAT SHE was everything his own mother should have been, and sometimes was, when her demons were giving her space. His father's generosity was something he took for granted when he was a child. He didn't regret his lack of appreciation. But he understood that unconditional love given freely and without strings was a very valuable thing. And he understood now, what Crystal wanted for Jenny.

Annie Trey walked past the garbage-pocked sidewalk in front of her building, and cut sideways into a park that would be relatively safe for two more hours. She peeped sideways at Jenny, pushing the stroller with her left hand, and covering her eyes with the right in the age-old game of peep-pie, a game every mother played with her child.

Jenny's laugh was a small, throaty gurgle, and David smiled till his face hurt. His cheeks felt stiff and cold, and the heat rose up in his chest with familiar tight flutters that felt like panic and pain.

Jenny pursed her lips and shut her eyes tight, covering them with chubby pink palms.

Annie Trey laughed and David knew that, at least for today, she saw the intense blue of dusk, not the haze of humidity and pollution. She would see the spring of grass that grew clumped and sparse in the poor, sandy soil, not the used condom and box of Jackie that lay squashed and oil-streaked at the base of the gutter. He knew too that the weeds that grew in the cracks of the sidewalk, flowering with wisps of soft, deep purple, were as good for her as roses.

Being a homicide cop was not about letting the killer go. It was not about playing judge and jury. Sometimes it was about seeing people get chewed up by a system that functioned with a thoughtlessness that was a crime all by itself. But it was the only system he had.

Annie pushed the stroller faster, executing a little hop and skip like the exuberant child that she was. David made up his mind.

Perhaps it was because he had the perspective of a dead man. He felt free not to follow the rules.

In his mind, the vision of Annie Trey skipping down the sidewalk warred with the image of Tina Cochran, holding her hands tight across her chest. He was sentencing her to years of pain.

But Luke Cochran was long dead, and Jenny had miles left to go.

He was going to go home. But first, he was going to buy Rose six new pair of white cotton socks, and candy and discs and silly things for his girls.

The car seemed a long way away.

His legs buckled, without warning, and he went down hard, but didn't feel a thing. He tried to get up, found it almost impossible to turn his head. He had the oddest sensation of sinking deeper and deeper into the ground. He looked for something pretty, something good to focus on, but he saw cigarette butts, and used condoms, and a trail of ants headed for something nasty. Someone called his name.

"Teddy?" he said.

"No, it's Valentine."

He opened his eyes, relieved to find something beautiful to look at. She looked worried. She was biting her lips.

"You got to get up," she told him. "Can't get those ambulances to come all the way out here."

"Don't worry," he told her. "Look after the girls and don't worry."

She was quick, he'd give her that. She'd always be quick.

"You didn't tell me Angie came by that night," he said. "No wonder you hated Luke. You knew, didn't you, Valentine?"

"I knew."

He was flooded with relief, she would talk to him.

"I want to know why he did it."

Her shrug was eloquent and dismissive. "Annie thought it was for the money. But you know what I think? I think he was mad. Annie's mama raised her not to have dealings with criminals. And she told him not to come around anymore." She touched his shoulder. "What you going to do?"

"I told you, don't worry. Leave it alone. Follow Eddie's advice. Don't say nothing about nothing. I won't."

She was talking to him, but it was too much of an effort to listen. He could see how relieved she was, surprised that they had been given a reprieve, and things had worked out for a change. He wondered how he could have ever thought she was less than beautiful.

The wail of the ambulance roused him. He found himself almost comfortable, a pillow under his head. He closed his eyes, smelling the starchy crisp smell of clean sheets, thinking that only Valentine could get an ambulance to come to Cracker Village.

FIFTY-FIVE

DAVID SAT QUIETLY IN THE SIDE ROOM OFF THE FOYER, listening to the rise and fall of voices, the rustle of clothes peculiar to a crowd of people dressed in their best. It felt strange to be out of the hospital. Strange to be back in the world.

He had been best man in name only, too weak to stand up with Mel for the necessary length of time.

He caught sight of Miriam, the off-the-shoulder ivory silk dress, the shine of long red hair across bare arms. Her belly rose round and firm and healthy, shielding the niece who would be born sometime around Christmas, if the doctors had called it right.

Miriam's cheeks were flushed, her eyes bright. He heard Mel's voice somewhere behind him, and Rose, sounding girlish and excited. Someone made a joke about brides wearing white like sacrificial lambs. Rose again? He should strangle her.

But Miriam was radiant, like all happy brides.

People were moving outside, to the tiny but steep rows of white steps in front of the church. It got quiet, and David's eyes felt heavy.

He did not want to sleep. He had had enough of sleeping.

He reached for the cane that sat on the chair beside him, took a breath, got slowly to his feet. It was hard to remember a time when he hadn't moved slowly. He hitched up his pants, waistband sagging, the collar of the starched white dress shirt loose on his neck.

One of the doors was partially open, a bright band of sunlight across the floor of the dim foyer. Outside, someone was laughing. David wanted to be outside, out in the sun, out with all the people.

He paced himself, doling out his strength. He heard Aslanti's voice in the back of his mind. He would know only gradually whether he would live or die, but it would be definite for him. All the way up or all the way down. He would grow weaker or stronger, inch by inch, till it became very clear whether he was moving ahead or falling behind.

He thought of how beautiful Teddy would look in ivory silk, and pictured himself, healthy and strong, moving down the aisle to meet her.

He made it out to the steps just as a shout went up, followed by a ripple of laughter. He took it in all at once—his little girls, dressed like angels, chasing each other across the lawn; Rose, blowing him a kiss. Miriam throwing her arms up, the flowers tumbling through the air, a pink rose petal trailing to the ground as String caught the bridal bouquet.

It was a moment of pure happiness, like oxygen to the heart, and he tried to tell himself that the tears in his eyes were caused by the sun.